BOUND

ICE WORLD WARRIORS : BOOK 2

JESSICA GRAYSON
ARIA WINTER

Purple Fall
Publishing

Published in the United States by Purple Fall Publishing. Purple Fall Publishing and the Purple Fall Publishing Logos are trademarks and/or registered trademarks of Purple Fall Publishing LLC.

Publisher's Cataloging-in-Publication data

Names: Grayson, Jessica, author. | Winter, Aria, author.

Title: Bound / Jessica Grayson and Aria Winter.

Series: Ice World Warriors

Description: Pleasanton, TX: Purple Fall Publishing, 2021.

Identifiers: ISBN

978-1-64253-063-6 (paperback)

978-1-64253-010-0 (ebook)

Subjects: LCSH Space exploration--Fiction. | Human-alien encounters--Fiction. | Vampires--Fiction. | Shapeshifting--Fiction. | Science fiction. | Romance fiction. | Paranormal fiction. | BISAC FICTION / Science Fiction / Alien Contact | FICTION / Romance / Science Fiction | FICTION / Romance / Paranormal / Shifters | FICTION / Romance / Fantasy | FICTION / Romance / Paranormal / Vampires

Classification: LCC PS3607 .R3978 B68 2021 | DDC 813.6--dc23

Cover Design by Maria Spada

DEDICATION

To my husband: You are not just my husband, you are my best friend and my rock. Thank you for all your love and support. I love you more than words can ever say.

-Jessica Grayson

CHAPTER 1

ALANA

A scream of pure terror echoes in my ears. My eyes snap open to pitch-black nothingness, my heart hammering as cold fear trickles down my spine. A thin beam of light shines in the distance. Focusing on it, I can just make out several dark shapes nearby, and I realize I'm still in my stasis pod on the ship, en route back to Terra from Mars.

Must be a stasis nightmare. I've had them before.

I blink several times, like that will somehow magically help me to see better in the darkness. Reaching forward, I tap the controls of my pod. The faint blue glow of the panel lights up, illuminating my reflection in the glass. My long blond hair is tied in a loose braid that hangs over my left shoulder. My blue eyes are half-lidded as I stare groggily at the screen.

It changes from calm blue to flashing red in warning. Alarm bursts through me, instantly clearing the fog from my brain.

Something is wrong.

I slam my hand on the emergency escape button. The restraint harness falls away as the pod door opens with a sharp hiss and drops to the floor.

My limbs feel heavy and uncoordinated as I struggle to pull myself out of my pod. Sweeping my gaze over the deck, I find six of my fellow crew members still in stasis, sleeping. The seventh—Harry—is not in his pod, but that's expected. We each take a rotation, a few weeks at a time, until we're less than a few days out from our destination, so one of us is always awake during the six-month long journey.

Why am I awake if the rest aren't?

As the ship's medical officer, I'm only supposed to be brought out of sleep early if someone needs medical help.

Harry.... Oh god, what if he's injured?

I half run, half stumble down the hallway.

"Harry!" I somehow manage to croak, my throat dry from who knows how long I've been asleep. "Where are you?"

No one answers. If Harry is hurt, he'll be in the med bay. The activation of the med scanner is what would trigger my pod to awaken me early—especially if it identified a condition needing immediate treatment.

"Harry!" I call out again, my voice echoing down the corridor. I round the corner, and my heart stops when I notice blood-smeared patterns along the metal floor and walls. Iron fills the air so thick I can taste it on my tongue.

One of the overhead lights hangs down at an odd angle, buzzing and flickering, casting sinister shadows as I pass.

Worry batters at my mind. Harry is my best friend.

It's my fault he's here in the first place.

He'd just broken up with his boyfriend, a month before their ship was set to leave for Terra. I found him a place on our crew, so he wouldn't be forced to spend so much time with the man who'd broken his heart.

Despite my fear, I force myself to continue, following the crimson trail down the hallway to the med center.

When I reach the doors, my jaw drops as I take in the several charred marks on the metal finish; they're pushed in, as if forced open. Quickly glancing inside, I notice Harry lying on the medical bed, covered in blood.

I squeak through the doors and rush to his side.

His face is pale and ashen. His blonde hair streaked red with blood, and his green eyes are wide as he takes in several, clipped, shallow breaths. "Harry, what happened to you?"

His head jerks toward the sound of my voice. Lightning fast, he curls his hand around my forearm in an iron grip, barely managing to wheeze. "They're here."

"Who?"

"You have to hide, Alana," he rasps. "They're coming back."

Panicked, I glance at the display readout. His wounds are severe, but treatable. "Harry, I can't just leave you here. You could—"

"Run," he grits through his teeth. "Hide."

A subtle hissing noise sounds behind me, sparking fear in my chest. Slowly, I spin to face it, and my mouth falls open when I see a strange, snake-like creature standing before me.

Two enormous, black eyes with yellow, vertically slit pupils stare back at me. It has a face like a cobra. The alien's lips pull back in a snarl, baring two large fangs.

It's covered in shiny, dark-crimson scales that appear coarse like sandpaper. His red-forked tongue flicks out as though tasting the air.

This creature is like something straight out of a nightmare. With two arms, two legs, and a long tail coiled behind it's body, its entire form is heavily muscled. Its three fingers are tipped with lethal, black claws.

Dressed in tight-fitting dark pants, the slight bulge

between its legs makes me think that this creature must be male.

Despite the primal fear twisting deep in my gut, I force myself into a defensive stance. Whatever this alien intends for us, I will not go down without a fight.

He rushes toward me, and I spin away. Kicking out with my left foot, I catch the back of his leg, knocking him off balance and sending him sprawling forward. He barely manages to catch himself before he falls. He growls and grips something on his belt, raising it toward me.

A blast of light flies past my head as I barely dodge it in time.

With no weapon of my own, I have only two options: run or fight.

Pushing down my fear, I charge toward the alien. His eyes are wide in shock as I kick out at the blaster in his hand, sending it flying across the room.

It hits the wall, bouncing off the metal panels and clattering across the floor.

I dive for it but too late.

A hand wraps around my ankle, jerking me back. I kick out blindly, making contact with something hard. A loud hiss fills the air, and the alien relinquishes his grip.

Scrambling across the floor, I grip the weapon firmly and twist onto my back to face my attacker.

He lunges for me, and I raise the weapon, depressing the first button I find. A blast of light races from the end of the barrel, hitting him square in the chest, sending him flying back.

He crumples to the ground, obsidian blood pooling around him. I watch, stunned, as the light slowly fades from his eyes.

"Alana! Look out!"

I spin to find three more snake-aliens behind me. I raise

my weapon to fire, but one of them beats me to it. A burst of light erupts from his blaster, and the world falls into slow motion as I throw myself in front of Harry to shield him.

Searing pain ripples along my back, and the world goes dark.

~

When I open my eyes, it's so dark in here, I can barely make out anything. I turn my head to the side.

In the low lighting I notice Harry lying next to me, both of us on a cold metal floor, surrounded by some sort of glowing energy field. "Harry?" I whisper urgently. "Harry, wake up."

His eyelids crack open. "Alana." He takes my hand weakly in his, squeezing it gently.

"Harry, are you all right?"

He bands his free arm across his torso, wincing as he slowly rolls onto his side. "Alana, where are we? What happened to the others?"

"I don't know."

"Over here," a voice calls out. "The cell across the way."

"You're Terran." I lift my head to find a woman with green eyes staring back at me, her long, blonde hair disheveled and pulled back in a loose knot at the base of her neck.

She looks so familiar, but I cannot place how I know her.

Tears roll down her cheeks. "I haven't seen another Terran in so long. My name is Abby. What's yours?"

"I'm Alana and this is Harry." I start to ask where we are, when the realization hits me. "Are you Abby Worthy?"

"Yes."

Harry's mouth drifts open. "Your ship disappeared seven years ago. How did—"

"It's been longer than that," Abby says, interrupting him.

5

"What do you mean?"

"My previous masters had a Healer scan me. He said I had been in stasis sleep for at least thirty to forty years."

I shake my head in disbelief. "No," I barely manage, "that can't be right."

It takes me a moment to compose myself, and when I finally do, despite my best efforts, my voice quavers as my eyes travel again over Abby's face. "I knew you looked familiar. How did you end up here? What happened to you and your crew?"

"I don't know. We went into stasis sleep on the journey back from Mars. But I woke up alone, in a cage."

"Do you know where we are? Where we're being taken?"

"We are being held until we reach one of the stations," someone interrupts.

My eyes dart in the direction of the unfamiliar voice, and my jaw drops when I find a pair of glowing, lavender eyes staring straight at me from across the way—in the same cell as Abby.

She appears just as stunned as I am that she's not alone.

He steps forward, and there's just enough light that I can make him out clearly now that he's moved out of the shadows at the back of their cell. He has two furry, white ears tipped with black—similar to what you'd see on a fox—peeking out from beneath his white hair.

"Please," Abby says, shrinking away from him. "Don't hurt me."

He turns to her. "Trust me. I am the least of your worries."

A long, white fox-like tail swishes behind him as he studies me with a piercing gaze. "What are you?" the question escapes my lips before I realize I've spoken it aloud.

"My name is Kyo. I'm a Kitsune." He dips his chin in a subtle nod, a sly grin curving his mouth. "And you three must be V'loryns, or..." his eyes travel over me, Harry and Abby, "something close, I presume."

"What's a V'loryn?"

He arches a brow. "Well, *this* is interesting." He cocks his head to the side to regard me. "I knew you looked a bit... off."

"I-I'm Terran," I reply. "So is my friend."

"Terran," he repeats. Sadness flits briefly across his features. "Yes. I have met one of your kind before. How did you get caught?"

"Our ship," Harry starts. "We were on our way back home when we were attacked. Most of our crew was in stasis sleep."

He nods. "It is the same story as the one I've heard from another of your kind. Perhaps, it's best you ran into me before we arrive."

"Why is that?" Harry asks, studying him warily.

"Because if anyone else finds out you are not V'loryn, your value drops. Significantly. You will be sold to less-than-savory characters, and I suspect you will not live out the end of the week, after that."

My heart stutters and stops. "We're slaves?"

He makes a point to sweep his gaze over the energy barrier. "What did you think we were?"

"I-I don't know...." My mind is going in several different directions at once while I process his words, my chest rising and falling rapidly as my heart pounds and races inside. "How do we escape?"

He arches a condescending brow. "If I had the answer, do you think I'd be here?"

Tears sting my eyes, but I blink them back. Harry wraps an arm around my shoulders. "It's all right, Alana. We'll figure something out."

"Forgive me for scaring you," Kyo says. "I mean you no harm, and I do not wish to cause you any undue stress. But, you must listen to me. If you want to survive, you must do exactly what I say."

"What do we need to do?"

He darts a glance at Abby, then back at me and Harry. "You must never tell anyone you are anything other than V'loryn. V'loryns are highly sought after and worth more on the slave trade than most other races. You two"—he gestures to me and Harry—"are you mates?"

"Mates?" Harry asks. "No, we're best friends."

Kyo purses his lips. "From now on, if anyone asks, you are a mated pair, do you understand?"

"Wha—" I start to ask, but he cuts me off.

"They're more likely to keep you together, if they believe you are mated. V'loryns bond for life. And you"—he looks to Abby—"we'll say you are with me. You must remember to keep your expressions neutral. The V'loryns are known for their lack of emotions."

He continues. "The V'loryns are similar to the A'kai, except they do not have green skin or white hair. Despite their lack of emotion, they detest slavery. If you come across one, they will help you to escape."

"Why would *you* help us?" Abby asks.

"I've seen enough suffering." His eyes brighten with unshed tears. "I used to keep to myself, but... not anymore. If I can help someone, I will."

"How do we know we can trust you?" Harry asks.

With a slight clench of his jaw, he lowers his gaze. "Because the one I love is Terran. She was taken from me, and I must get her back."

He turns to Abby, dipping his chin in a subtle bow. "I vow I will never harm you. I will do everything I can to keep you safe. I swear it to the stars and the Fates."

An echoing thud sounds along the hull, and the ship rocks slightly back and forth. "We must have docked," Kyo says. He looks to each of us. "Remember what I've told you. You can survive, but you must be smart. Anguis slavers are known for their cruelty, but they are also known to be business savvy. They will not kill you lightly. You are too valuable. Do not anger them."

"Anguis?"

A pained smile ghosts his lips. "Anna always referred to them as snake-aliens."

I open my mouth to ask him more about Anna, but several Anguis walk in.

I notice two different aliens with them. Taller than any Terran I've ever seen, they have sharp, pointed ears like elves, long, silver-white or black hair, pale-green skin, sharp, angular features, and three slightly raised cranial ridges that start from between their brows—one that goes straight up their forehead and the other two that spread out like a *V* to either temple.

My jaw drops. "They look so much like—" I start to say: "like the man I dream of," but stop short.

"A'kai," Kyo whispers urgently. "Yes, they look like V'loryns, but they are very different."

V'loryns. I commit this word to memory as I think on the man I've seen in my dreams almost every night for the past five years.

Kyo looks to Harry. "We must hide the females."

Kyo pulls Abby behind him while Harry does the same to me.

It doesn't matter, however.

Dressed from head to toe in some sort of form-fitting, black armor, their glowing, green eyes study Harry and me with a piercing stare.

Glancing at Kyo, I observe as all the color drains from his face as he stands protectively in front of Abby, trying to shield her from them.

"We'll take those two." One of them points to our cell.

One of the Anguis bows low. "Of course, Lord Novan. I guarantee you will be pleased."

He growls. "Do you have any more like these?"

The Anguis darts a glance toward Kyo and Abby's cell. "How much will you pay for them?"

The A'kai's eyes go pitch-black, and his canines extend into sharp, pointed tips as his nails lengthen into deadly claws.

My heart thunders in my chest. "Vampire," I whisper under my breath, staring at them in shock.

Novan wraps his hand around the Anguis's neck, lifting him off the ground as if he weighs nothing. "Consider them a gift to the A'kai Empire."

The Anguis opens his mouth, but only a choked gurgling sound escapes him. He barely manages to nod. The A'kai relinquishes his grip and the Anguis drops like a stone to the floor.

He quickly recovers and turns to us. He removes some sort of rod from his belt. When he taps the end on the floor, a low buzzing hum fills the air and electricity sparks at the end. "If you give me any trouble, I'll hit you with the shock stick," he hisses.

He opens the cage and grasps my forearm to drag me out. Despite his threat, I struggle to free myself as Harry rushes him.

Lightning fast, the Anguis hits him with the shock stick.

Harry's mouth opens in a silent scream and he drops to the floor.

"*No!*" I jerk my arm free and fall to my knees at Harry's side, taking his hand in mine.

The Anguis wraps his hand around my upper arm. His scaled palm is rough like sandpaper against my skin as I kick and scream as he tries to pull me away. I hold tightly to

Harry's hand, his eyelids fluttering open and closed. "Harry!"

Something hard stabs at my side. Pain explodes across my torso as electricity arcs through my body like fire. The world goes black, and I fall away into darkness.

Strong arms wrap around me and I know this can't be real, but I don't care. The man I've dreamed of almost every night for the past five years smooths a hand down my back as he holds me against the solid warmth of his chest. His glowing green eyes stare deep into mine and there is no mistaking the love reflected behind them.

I tip my head up to his, studying the features of this man I know so well. I cup his cheek, as my gaze travels over his face. His aristocratic nose and features and his masculine, square jaw that could cut glass, make him appear both proud and fiercely handsome.

His hair is short-cropped and raven-black—a sharp contrast to his otherwise pale skin. His ears have pointed, elvish tips. I scan the sharp lines of his brow and the three cranial ridges originating from between his brows. One goes straight up the center of his forehead to his hairline, and the other two extend in a V-shape toward his temples.

He looks so much like our cruel A'kai masters, but without their green skin and white hair. Despite how similar they appear, I know he cannot be one of them. He's too kind and too caring.

When I first began dreaming of him, long ago, I used to think he was strange. But not anymore. He is ethereally handsome as he stares down at me; too perfect to be real.

"Are you a V'loryn?" I ask, but he does not answer. Instead, he takes my hand and places it over his heart.

"Si'an T'kara," he whispers the soft and lilting words.

And although I do not know what these words mean, I under-

stand their meaning in the way they leave his lips in a breathless whisper. These are words that need no translation to be understood. They resonate deep in my soul.

"You are the reason," I whisper against his chest. "Sometimes, I feel like it would be easier just to give up. But then I think of you. I wonder if you are real and waiting for me somewhere. You are the hope that keeps me alive." A tear slips down my cheek. "I know you are only a dream, but will you stay with me for a while longer?"

His green gaze holds mine intently. "Always, my Si'an T'kara."

It feels like forever since we were sold, and I haven't seen Harry in all that time. In space, it is almost impossible to tell time without the rising and setting of a sun to indicate the start and end of each day. I'm not even sure Harry's alive. One of the other Terran girls said she thinks she may have seen him when she was first brought on board, but she isn't sure. The description sounds close enough, however, that it gives me hope.

I pull my knees up to my chest and curl into a ball. Closing my eyes, I dream of home: of blue skies and green forests and white puffy clouds—bright and vivid colors now existing only in my memories. Images that seem so far away and too perfect to have ever been real.

A strong hand grips my chin, and I gasp as Novan's glowing, green eyes meet mine. "Show me your home world."

"No," I whisper. "I won't."

Blood rushes through my ears, drowning out all other sounds, as pressure grows in the back of my mind like water readying to burst forth from a dam.

Without warning, the barrier of my mind crumbles. The full force of his consciousness invades and expands in my mind.

I'm drowning in darkness, the crushing weight of his consciousness bearing down upon my own. The razor-sharp lash of his thoughts whips at my mind as he takes command of my body with unyielding brutality in the *R'ugol*—the forced mind link.

This is why the A'kai are so feared. Staring at the cruel lines of his face, I watch his glowing, green eyes turn into obsidian orbs. He rips through my thoughts, tearing open my memories as he searches for what he wants: the location of Terra.

I throw up images of Mars like a barrier between us, hoping to confuse him. Gritting my teeth, I focus on the memories of the red, barren planet. It's nothing like home, and I want him to believe my people come from a dying world and that there aren't many of us left.

A sinister growl rumbles his chest. "Do. Not. Fight. Me."

Panic steals my breath as he leans down to scent me, grazing his fangs along the curve of my neck. Goosebumps prickle my flesh as something warm and wet drags across my skin, directly over my pulsing artery.

His dark desire floods my mind, and I choke on a scream as he sinks his teeth deep into my neck. The heavy scent of iron fills the air so thick I taste it on my tongue.

The sick pull against my skin is agonizing torture as he drinks of my blood. His hands clamp down on my arms in a bruising grip, and I'm unable to move, his consciousness holding mine prisoner.

"That's enough," a dark voice sounds behind him. "You'll kill her, if you take any more."

Weak from blood loss, I can barely lift my head when he reluctantly pulls away. I was moments away from falling away into the beckoning void of oblivion.

Across the room, I hear a terrified whimper as another

A'kai sinks his teeth deep into Violet's neck. Her green eyes lock onto mine, full of fear, as he drinks of her blood.

She beats her fists against him a moment before her head falls back and she goes limp.

"Stop it!" I cry out. "You'll kill her!"

He jerks away from her, his fangs dripping with blood as he levels an icy glare at me. "You," he snarls, "do not tell me—"

"She's right," another A'kai snaps. "We cannot take too much. The Captain was furious after that Terran female died a few days ago."

Novan releases me and I rush toward Violet. I drop to my knees beside her and take her hand. "Violet?"

Her eyelids flutter open and closed as she turns her head to me. "Alana," she whispers. "Thank you."

Tears sting my eyes as I stare down at my friend. I swallow against a lump in my throat as I think of Sarah. I held her hand like this as she faded away. There was nothing I could do. They'd taken too much of her blood when they drank from her.

I carefully brush the hair back from Violet's face and then discreetly check the pulse on her neck.

Weakly, she squeezes my hand. "Will I be all right?"

"As long as they don't take anymore."

"I felt myself fading away," she whispers, as a tear slips down her cheek. "I was so scared."

I turn and three pairs of glowing green eyes snap to me. Tipping my chin up, I feign a bravery that I do not feel in this moment as I force myself to stare down the monsters that keep us as slaves. "You cannot drink from her anymore," I state, struggling to hide the trembling in my voice. "She is too weak and needs time to recover."

Another A'kai—Falen—stalks toward me and I raise my arms, trying to shield myself and Violet. His people have two to three times the strength of a Terran. The last time he hit me, I was unconscious for two days.

"Fine," he snarls. He gathers me in his arms while another does the same to Violet. "Let's take them back to their cages. We have plenty of slaves to choose from on this ship."

A shiver goes down my spine at his words as we start back to the cargo bay, while another one carries Violet behind us.

She was in the Terran space program too—just like the rest of us, the last thing she remembers is going into stasis and waking up in a cage.

Another A'kai crosses the hallway up ahead, and I inhale sharply when I notice a man with blond hair being dragged behind him with a slave collar and chain. His gaze is trained on the floor, but from his height and build, he looks so much like Harry.

I open my mouth to shout out to him, but quickly snap it shut. Doing so would only bring unwanted attention from the A'kai.

The man's eyes snap up to meet mine a moment before we enter the cargo bay. Despite his gaunt appearance, his green eyes are so familiar. I notice the spark of recognition that flickers across his expression.

Hope blooms deep inside me. I'm certain it's Harry.

The doors slide shut behind us, plunging me into darkness. The A'kai are predators, and from what I've gleaned from Novan's mind during our connection, his world is one of perpetual night. His people prefer the dark, but I know they are able to tolerate the light, as well, so it cannot be used against them as a weakness.

He throws me into my cage, pausing a moment to lift a lock of my long, blonde hair to his nose and inhale deeply. He could force himself on me anytime he wanted—taking my body the same way he takes my mind. But he waits,

15

claiming someday I'll ask him on my own—that I'll worship him as both lover and master.

My body begins trembling involuntarily at the thought. It is only a matter of time before he loses patience and simply takes what he wants.

Tears sting my eyes and blur my vision as I curl onto my side, hugging my knees to my chest.

"Alana?" Lara's soft voice calls out in the darkness.

Although I cannot see, I know she is in the cage beside mine. I raise my hand, placing my open palm against the grating and feel hers touch mine a moment later, and I thread my fingers through hers.

Lara is like a sister to me. We served on the same ship. We've been friends since flight school. I could hardly believe it when I was brought on board and she was already here. I was so afraid I'd never see any of my crew again.

"Are you all right?" she asks.

A tear slips down my cheek, but I quickly brush it away. I'm not all right, and deep down, I fear that even if we, somehow, manage to escape from this place... I never will be again.

"I keep hoping I'll wake back up on the ship," my voice quavers. "That I'll awaken to realize this was all just a terrible dream in the stasis pod. That we're on our way home to Terra." I pause. "I saw him, Lara. I saw Harry. He's here on the ship."

"Are you sure?"

"Yes. It was only a glimpse, but I know it was him."

I shudder as I think on some of the other slaves I've seen on this vessel. The A'kai consider Terran females valuable and do not drink from us as often as they do the males and other races they keep here on their ship.

Lara squeezes my hand. "At least we know he's alive."

"He's my best friend," my voice quavers softly. "I should have fought harder. I should have—"

"Shhhh," she soothes. "You did everything you could."

"You saw Harry?" Violet asks weakly. "I knew, from your description, that I was right. It *was* him, wasn't it?"

"Yes," I reply. "That means there are more of us—more Terrans—being held on a different part of the ship, somewhere."

I suspect the A'kai have dozens of slaves on board and probably keep them in several different cargo holds.

I'm trying to be strong, but each time they enter my mind is worse than the last. I'm so afraid I'll lose myself and become some mindless automaton that does their bidding.

"We have to find a way to get out of here," Lara says.

"Where will we go?" Violet asks. "We don't even know where we are."

"Do you have a plan, Lara?" Mina's voice whispers in the darkness.

"We just have to get out of here," Elain's voice quavers. "Even if we die trying, it would be better than living like this."

"What if—" Violet starts, but stops as a piercing, high-pitched whine screeches through the ship.

The sound of metal grinding against metal is quickly followed by a deafening boom rippling along the hull. The ship rocks violently to one side, and pain explodes across my torso as I slam against the cage bars.

The doors whoosh open, and one of the A'kai races into the cargo bay. Red lights flash behind him in the hallway, and sirens blare in warning.

He flips a switch and the cage locks snap open. "Get out!" he yells. "We're evacuating!"

"What's going on?" someone asks.

17

"We're being pulled through a worm hole," he barks. "It's tearing apart the ship."

A voice drones over the speakers. "Five minutes until hull integrity failure."

"Move!" he snarls. "We have to go!"

We scramble out of our cages and follow after him as he races down the corridor. It's been so long since I've run, my muscles ache in protest as we follow.

The A'kai move with lightning speed, and it's difficult to keep up. My calves begin to cramp, but Lara takes my hand, pulling me along behind her. Her light blue eyes are wide, and her chestnut hair is wild around her face, having escaped her long braid. "We have to keep going."

Everything is chaos as A'kai soldiers rush past us, everyone racing to the escape pods.

"Evacuate the Terrans!" the Captain roars. "Leave the others!"

My gaze slides to a Kitsune slave being dragged along behind another A'kai by her collar. He drops the chain and heads straight for our group. Horror stops my heart as I realize they're not going to evacuate all of the slaves. Just us, because we're more valuable to them. They claim our blood has restorative properties for their race.

Rounding a corner, we enter into a massive room lined with what I can only guess are escape pods. They look like they should only fit one person, but I watch A'kai soldiers file into them in pairs.

"I need one soldier for every Terran," one of them commands.

Several of the A'kai's heads snap in our direction, and I note how eagerly many of them move toward us.

They're probably all thinking the same thing. Since we have no idea what awaits us after escaping the ship, they must be speculating how great it would be to have readily available food, when they land.

I sweep my gaze over the entire area, searching desperately for any sign of Harry, but I see none. It's obvious, however, that our cargo bay wasn't the only one full of Terran women. Many unfamiliar faces file past me, each of them as scared and surprised to see us as we are them.

As I observe Terran women being grabbed by A'kai soldiers and thrown into escape pods, reality suddenly hits me.

I'm going to be separated from Lara.

I throw my arms around her neck, holding her tight.

I cannot lose her.

Not Lara. Warm tears escape my lashes as I hug her. "I don't want to leave you."

"I don't either—"

Her words are cut short as an A'kai jerks her away.

I scream as an arm bands around my waist, dragging me toward one of the pods. I kick out, fighting and desperate to free myself, as I watch Lara being taken.

"Be still!" Novan's harsh voice commands. "Or I'll kill you and be done with it!"

I stop struggling when he throws me into a seat and tightens the harness. The straps dig into my flesh as he secures them before strapping into the seat beside me.

The control panel lights up, and I watch as he taps a series of symbols on the screen. A green light flashes in the corner. With a loud rush of air, the pod violently ejects, tumbling away from the ship and out into the dark void of space.

I watch several others fly past us, the massive A'kai vessel growing smaller in the viewscreen, as we spin away.

A blinding, yellow-orange flash fills the viewscreen when the A'kai ship explodes in a brilliant display of light.

A shockwave spreads out from the explosion and rushes

toward us. I only have a moment to brace myself, gripping the handrails tightly, before it hits.

The pod shakes and spirals through the darkness. I swallow against the bile rising in my throat from the turbulent spinning as alarms blare through the speakers.

Red lights fill the cabin as the display flashes several bright symbols. I'm not sure what they are, but from Novan's panicked expression, I know it cannot be good.

A gray-blue planet appears in the distance, covered in clouds.

The hull creeks and groans as the pod begins to descend into the upper atmosphere. A wall of flame flares brightly outside the viewscreen, heating the interior and searing my skin.

We're going to burn up before we reach the surface.

I squeeze my eyes shut and think of home, and the last time I saw the blue-green of Terra.

Novan releases a string of curses and I open my eyes.

An icy landscape, full of snow-capped trees that remind me of the great pines of Terra, races toward us. The hull scrapes along the top and crashes through them, jerking violently, carving a path through the dense forest as we descend.

A thunderous boom explodes through the cabin as we hit the ground, and my world goes dark.

CHAPTER 2

VOREK

Early morning light filters in through the window, casting a soft, orange glow throughout the room. It reminds me of my home world—V'lora, and I wonder if I will ever see it again.

Sitting up, I run a hand through my short, black hair and stand. I walk over to the cleansing room and turn on the shower. We are fortunate, at least, that everything still functions on our crashed ship.

Everything but the engines, that is.

If those were working, we'd have left this planet long ago.

Still, we are fortunate compared to the others who are stranded on this world. It is a testimony to V'loryn engineering that we still have the use of our technology on our vessel.

The warm water flows over me like a soothing balm, relaxing some of the tension in my neck and shoulders. After I encountered Markus in the forest yesterday, I found it difficult to sleep.

Despite the fact that he is Mosauran, he and I used to be as close as brothers. With a heavy sigh, I shake my head.

But, that was long ago, and much has changed since then.

Before yesterday, he and I had not spoken in several turns of the moon.

The female he was with appeared so similar to our people, I thought at first she was V'loryn. Her name was Lara, and she said she is Terran—a race I have never heard of before.

I cannot deny my shock when Markus claimed her as his. Mosaurans are like us: they do not take mates outside of their race.

She claimed she and several of her kind evacuated a slave ship, each of them forced into a two-person escape pod with an A'kai.

She said there were at least twenty Terran females, including herself, on that ship, which means at least that many A'kai landed here, as well, if not more.

The A'kai are as dangerous as they are lethal—one of the few races evenly matched to my own. It is believed we share a common ancestor. Our appearances are similar except that they have green skin and white hair. But, that is where all the similarity ends. The A'kai still hold to the old ways. They are blood drinkers, whereas my people gave up that practice over a thousand cycles ago. An increase in their numbers on this world could be devastating.

This is troubling news. We have been stranded on this planet for the past five cycles and surrounded by enemies. The A'kai, the Lycaons and the Mosaurans. All of our ships were pulled through that blasted wormhole while we were fighting.

At least the Aerilon are not our enemies. Our alliance with them here has only made our position and our territory that much stronger against possible invasion by the others.

Stepping out of the shower, I wrap a towel around my hips and move to the sink. My glowing, green eyes reflect back at me as I study myself in the mirror. I scrub a hand across the short scruff of beard outlining my jaw and decide against shaving it this day.

I have too much to attend to bother with it. Besides, my brother Tavek is usually clean shaven, so it will be easier for everyone to tell us apart, this way. Although he is three cycles younger than me, people often mistake us for twins.

Thinking again on the Terrans and their captors—the A'kai—my thoughts drift to the memory of my sister, L'yra. She was enslaved and her mind violated in the R'ugol by their evil race. Curling my hands into fists, my fangs extend into sharpened points, rage churning deep in my gut.

I am the oldest. It was my responsibility to watch over her, after the death of our parents, and I failed.

Closing my eyes, I force myself to push aside the painful memories of L'yra's death and will myself to calm. The A'kai are monsters, and I can hardly bear the thought there are potentially several more females on this world enslaved by them.

I change into my dark uniform—tunic, pants, and matching boots—then start for the door. As soon as I step out into the hallway, I notice my brother, Tavek, leaving his room.

His gaze travels over my face, and he arches a brow. "Are you feeling unwell?"

With a heavy sigh, I purse my lips. Tavek knows me so well. It has always been this way between us. "I could not sleep. I was thinking of L'yra."

"I was unable to sleep, too. Your... meeting yesterday with Commander Markus, and the Terran female he rescued, brought back all the memories of L'yra. It has been many cycles, but—" his voice catches.

I place a hand on his shoulder. "I know, Brother."

"Vorek!"

I turn and find Al'iro walking toward us, his wings tucked close to his back. At least they are not fluttering in agitation —a telltale sign among his people, the Aerilons, when they are upset. He dips his chin in polite greeting to Tavek, then turns his attention back to me. His golden eyes meet mine evenly. "I want to go with you today."

I shake my head. "You must stay here."

He opens his mouth to protest, but I quickly add, "You are one of only two Healers. We cannot afford to risk you. Besides, with more A'kai on the planet, it is imperative we guard our territory. We cannot spread ourselves too thin in our search and leave what we have here unprotected."

"It would be best if more of *my* people went out in the search," he counters. "Our ability to fly would make it much easier, if we found any of the Terran females, to bring them back here to treat them."

What he says makes sense, and I would agree, if not for the Mosaurans. I sigh heavily. "The Mosaurans are volatile and aggressive, and more importantly, they have wings just like your people. If you and other Aerilon are out searching for Terrans, we lose the only other advantage we have against the Mosaurans—the ability to meet them in the air, if they approach without warning."

His pale-violet skin darkens slightly in anger, and he runs a hand roughly through his short, dark hair as his wings flutter behind him in agitation. "Since when do you speak for my people?"

I arch a brow at his challenging words. "I do not claim to. I only strive to be a voice of reason... of caution. You have always trusted my counsel in the past. Does it count for nothing now?"

"That was different," he replies, but in his eyes it is easy to read that he understands. He remembers how often I have saved him and my brother from charging into a situation and getting themselves killed.

"He is right," Tavek says beside me. "As much as I dislike the idea of staying here when there are those who are suffering at the hands of the A'kai, we must keep some of our people here, in case they decide to invade our territory and take what we have."

"When we find the females, we will need a place for them to rest and shelter," I tell him. "If we lose this ship, and all its technology, what will we have to offer them then?"

Al'iro gives me a reluctant look and claps a hand on my shoulder. "Forgive me, Vorek. You know I consider you a brother. Both of you." He shifts his gaze to Tavek. "I just... I can hardly bear the thought of anyone suffering under the A'kai."

I understand his anger. He lost a sister as well because of the A'kai. It is the common thread between us—our shared hatred of their vile race—that led to our alliance on this world.

"I feel the same, my friend. I only ask that you consider my counsel. We cannot commit everyone to this search. We must leave behind enough to defend our territory."

With a slight clench of his jaw, Al'iro nods. He taps his wristband communicator and looks to mine. "Promise me you will, at least, stay in range so you might reach us, should you have a problem."

I cannot promise this. There is an ore beneath the ground that impairs communication equipment. "I will try."

Al'iro glances out a nearby window. "The skies are clear for now, but that could easily change."

I send a silent prayer to the goddess that the weather will hold while we search. Storms here can be rather unpredictable and last anywhere from hours to several days. This also causes signal disruptions on our communicators. "I will leave now and return before nightfall."

~

Making my way through the forest, I cannot stop thinking of the Terran female—Lara—who was with Commander Markus. She looked so much like one of my own people, I was almost certain she was V'loryn.

But, she is smaller than our females, and I worry for her kin. Only a few nights ago, I witnessed several A'kai escape pods descending from the upper atmosphere.

That is why we have increased our patrols—the A'kai are dangerous. To know they have slaves with them fills me with dread.

I cannot imagine a fate worse than being owned by one of their kind.

I draw in a deep breath as I scent the air for any sign of the females or the A'kai, the cold air burning my lungs with each inhalation. Flakes of snow dance and twirl on the breeze, blanketing the land in a fresh layer of white and decreasing my chances of finding any tracks as I search.

My people are so similar in appearance to the A'kai, I am concerned the Terran females may fear us, just as Lara did when she first saw me.

The A'kai are blood drinkers and the conditions on this ice world are harsh. I worry they will begin feeding on their slaves for survival. This thought lends speed to my steps, and I send another prayer to the goddess to help us find and rescue the Terrans as soon as possible.

As I make my way through the woods, a scream pierces the air—the pure terror in its pitch raising the hair on the back of my neck.

I scan the forest, searching for any sign of movement, but

notice nothing.

Another scream echoes through the trees, and I run toward it.

Racing across the snow-covered landscape, I crunch through the icy snow, probably alerting every creature within several *arcums* of my location, but I do not care.

In the far distance, I notice an A'kai escape pod. The design and the dark, metallic hull unmistakable against the stark white landscape and pale, gray-blue sky.

Downwind from the wreckage, a cool breeze blows across the ice, and my nostrils flare, catching the bittersweet scent of blood in the air. A female runs from around the side of the A'kai vessel. With pale skin and long, blonde hair, she appears V'loryn.

An A'kai soldier chases her, his fangs bared as he moves toward her like a predator stalking its prey.

My heart hammers as I charge toward her. The powdery snow is like shifting sand beneath my boots as I struggle to reach her, desperate to save her from the A'kai.

She turns back to face him, appearing ready to stand and fight.

What is she doing?

The A'kai rushes toward her, and she spins away, kicking out with her left foot.

She makes contact, and he stumbles back, roaring his anger.

He recovers quickly and lunges forward, catching her around the waist.

A panicked scream escapes her lips, but it is quickly cut off as he slams her back against the hull. She crumples to the ground.

Rage burns through my veins as I race toward them. My canines extend into sharpened points, my nails into deadly claws. He will pay for daring to harm her.

Unaware of me, as I rush toward them through the woods, he dips his head to the curve of her neck and shoulder, readying to feed off her blood.

An angry roar rips from my throat.

His head jerks back and whips in my direction. He releases his grip on the female a moment before I crash into him.

We tumble through the snow in a tangled mess of limbs, fangs, and claws. He reaches for his blaster, but I kick it away.

We both scramble to our feet. His glowing, green eyes swirl with black as they lock on mine, full of rage. Obsidian blood stains the snow as we circle one another, dripping from our many wounds.

"I know what you are thinking, V'loryn," he snarls. "But she is not one of yours."

"It matters not," I grit through my teeth. "I will not allow you to harm her."

The A'kai narrows his eyes. "We are not so different, you and I." His gaze sweeps over the icy landscape. "We can each survive on her blood for many days. On a planet such as this, a reliable food source is a blessing, is it not?"

"My people are not savage like yours. You *will not* touch her."

His lips pull back in a feral grin, revealing long, sharp fangs. "Then, I will have no choice but to kill you, V'loryn."

"You may try" —I growl, baring my fangs in return—"but you will not succeed."

Lightning fast, he lunges toward me.

I twist away, but his claws catch my torso. Blinding pain shoots through me as they rake across my skin.

I force myself to ignore the pain, and charge toward him. His gaze darts to the left, and that is all the sign I need to predict his next move.

He tries to feign right, but I already know his intent. I slash my claws across his throat, and he drops to his knees.

His eyes are wide as he clutches at his neck, trying to stem the bleeding of his mortal wound. It spills down his front and pools in the snow around him. He opens his mouth to speak, but only a choked, gurgling noise escapes, and he falls to the side.

I watch in cold satisfaction as the light fades from his eyes. "You will never harm anyone again," I grind out.

I glance down at my communicator, pursing my lips in frustration when I realize I have no signal out here.

Turning back to the female, I find her still on the ground, propped up against the hull of the escape pod.

I kneel before her. "Are you all right?"

She lifts her gaze. Luminous blue eyes meet mine, and my heart stutters and stops. My lips part, but I am unable to speak, much less form a coherent thought.

Si'an'inamora.

The ancient V'loryn words echo in my mind, and my world shifts in an instant.

She is my *Si'an T'kara*—my fated one.

"I think so," she barely manages, her eyes wide.

I stare in awestruck wonder at the female before me. How is it possible that my fated mate is not V'loryn? It has been over two thousand cycles since anyone was blessed with the fated bond, and it has never happened outside of our race.

Pale, blonde hair hangs over her shoulders in long, silken waves. She gently tucks a stray tendril behind her ear, and I note the gentle curve of her ears where a V'loryn's would be pointed. Her forehead is smooth where my people have three slight cranial ridges. Her skin is covered in a fine dusting of spots, and her eyes are a fascinatingly vivid shade of blue.

She is much smaller than one of our females, and she has the same eyes, hair, and pale skin as the one I saw with

Commander Markus. He said she was Terran. I suspect this female is, as well, but I must be sure.

"What species are you?"

"Terran," she replies. "Are you V'loryn?"

"Yes." I study her. "Have you come across others of my kind?"

She shakes her head. "I was told that your people look like the A'kai, but without the green skin and white hair."

"Yes. It is believed we share a common ancestor with the A'kai, but my people do not follow their ways. We are not savage like them."

She lifts her eyes to mine, but she says nothing. Perhaps she is weighing whether or not to trust me.

I do not have much time to try to convince her.

We are exposed out here. I do not know if there are any more A'kai nearby, and I do not wish to find out. I will simply have to show her I mean her no harm through my actions.

"I am Vorek. I will take care of you. You are safe with me. I swear it to the stars. My vow."

She reaches her small and delicate right hand out to me. "I'm Alana. Thank you for saving me."

She wants to touch me? My eyes widen in shock and I swallow thickly, uncertain of how to proceed.

"I am Vorek of House H'laeth." I dip my chin in a subtle acknowledgment of her thanks and am relieved when she lowers her arm back down to her side.

Her tattered slave dress and skin are spattered with obsidian blood. Studying the dark bruise marks on her neck and arms, something catches the corner of my eye, and I watch as a line of red liquid trails down from a tear in her scalp on her forehead.

My people are touch telepaths, able to transmit and receive thoughts and emotions through the simple act of touch. It is forbidden to touch one to whom you are not bonded through marriage or family.

But she is injured.

I am careful to maintain my mental shields—to prevent the transmission of thought and emotion—when I reach out to touch the liquid dripping onto her cheek. My brow furrows deeply. "You bleed red?"

"Yes."

"I will take you back to my people. We have Healers that can treat you. We must hurry if we are going to reach them before nightfall."

"Wait," she says. "I have to find my friends. There may be more of us out here and—"

"I know. I ran into one of them a few days ago."

She blinks several times. "You did?"

"Yes, I—"

A low howl sounds in the distance, followed by a chorus of others. The hair rises on the back of my neck. "The Lycaons are close. We must hurry."

"Lycaons?"

"Yes. They hunt in packs. We must leave here before they find us. Can you run?"

She pushes up on one hand but cries out sharply, hissing between gritted teeth as she collapses back onto the snow in pain.

My heart stops. "Where are you hurt?"

She carefully lifts her left arm from her side, revealing an injury on her torso. Anger floods my veins as I take in the angry red slash marks made by the claws of an A'kai.

"It's all right." She winces as she struggles to sit up straight. "I just need to clean it and bandage it so it won't get infected."

Wisps of snow flutter on the breeze all around us as I study her injuries. Her skin is petal-soft compared to mine.

Already my wounds are beginning to close, but hers do not show any signs of healing.

Worry fills me as a rolling boom of thunder sounds in the distance. Glancing over my shoulder, I observe the dark clouds gathering nearby. The tempests on this world are as dangerous and can appear rather suddenly.

Some last for only a few hours, but others can last days, and it is difficult to tell which this one will be. All I know for certain is that it lies between us and the direction we must travel to reach my people.

Glancing down at her, another chorus of howls fills the air, and dread trickles down my spine. Even without the storm, the Lycaons are close, and I am not sure I can outrun them, if I must carry Alana.

I cannot risk taking her through the storm. Not if it is going to turn into a blizzard. Already, her small form shivers.

It seems her species is not able to regulate their body temperatures as effectively as mine. Then again, it may also be because she is injured. I remove the heavy, fur cloak from my shoulders and wrap it around her. "This should help keep you warm."

"Thank you," she murmurs, tugging it closer around her.

I want to get her to the Healers, but that may not be possible, if we are caught in the storm. So, I must search for something to use for her injuries, in case we are unable to make it back to my territory, before the weather gets worse.

The first thing we learn in our training on the V'loryn Defense Force is to make use of whatever is at hand—especially during an emergency situation. We must be able to adapt and overcome whatever obstacle is laid out before us.

I look to the A'kai vessel. If it is like most escape pods, it will probably have an emergency med kit.

My eyes sweep over the icy terrain surrounding us, searching for any sign of danger, but it seems we are alone out here. For now. The Lycaons either do not know we are here or they are still far enough away they are not an immediate threat.

"I must search for an emergency kit. We need to tend your wounds before you lose more blood. Wait here. I will return quickly."

"Trust me, I'm not going anywhere." She grimaces slightly as she tries to move. "I'll wait right here."

Alana may be small, but she is brave and strong of will. Despite that he was much larger and stronger than her, she tried to fight the A'kai. I have seen males in battle with injuries far less serious than hers who have cried out like wild *katirs*. And yet, she bears her pain in silence.

I turn toward the A'kai vessel and climb up into the hatch, carefully lowering myself inside.

Making my way quickly through the cabin, I search each compartment for a med kit or something to bind over her wounds. When I find a blaster in one of the cabinets, I tuck it into my belt. Weapons are valuable on this goddess-forsaken planet.

A heavy sigh of relief escapes me when I finally locate the emergency kit and find medical supplies, including an unused tube of healing gel inside, along with two thermal blankets, several nutrient bars, and water packs.

Slinging the supply pack over my shoulder and across my chest, I climb back out of the hatch. Upon reaching the ground, I turn to face Alana, studying her with shock and renewed admiration. While I was gone, she managed to pull herself to standing, despite her painful injuries.

When she takes a step, she stumbles forward.

I catch her in my arms before she falls, and her eyes flick to mine.

"Allow me to carry you."

"I can walk."

A piercing chorus of howls sounds from the forest. "Please, let me carry you. We must leave here before the Lycaons find us."

Her eyes are wide with fear as she nods in agreement.

Wrapping my arms around her smaller form, I lift her to my chest, surprised at how slight her weight is compared to my people.

Tightening my hold around her, I break into a run, praying to the goddess I can outrace the Lycaons, and the storm, to make it to the pass between the mountains. From there, I should be able to reach my people with my communicator to call for help.

Snow and ice crunch beneath my feet as I race through the woods at my full V'loryn speed.

Would that I had wings like Al'iro or the rest of his Aerilon crew.

The wind picks up, pulling at my form and trying to rip Alana from my arms, as heavy snow begins to fall all around us. The white flakes whirl and spin so thick I can barely make out what is in front of me. I slow my pace considerably, unable to see clear enough to keep running.

With her head tucked under my chin, Alana buries her face in my chest as her entire body shivers. I must find shelter, and soon. My Si'an T'kara cannot be out in the cold like this for much longer.

Scanning the area immediately around us for a familiar landmark, I breathe a sigh of relief when I realize we are close to one of our scout caves.

When we first crashed on this planet a little over five cycles ago, we made regular patrols of the territory surrounding our ship. Because we are not the only ones stranded here, it was important to guard against our enemies: the A'kai, the Mosauran and the Lycaons.

My people have formed a treaty with the Aerilon to work

and live together, but we have no such arrangement with the Lycaons and the Mosaurans. They are too volatile and aggressive to ever even consider this. And the A'kai are savage and evil. We would never ally ourselves with them.

Something moves in the shadows at the edge of my vision, the heavy snowfall making it difficult to discern what it is. Dread twists deep in my gut as I scent the wind, praying to the goddess it is not an enemy. If it is, I do not know if I could defend Alana and fight them off at the same time.

I go still, crouching behind a large boulder. We are at the base of the mountain, and it is not far to the cave, but I am reluctant to go there just yet. If I were alone, I would be certain I could outrun whatever this is, but I have Alana, which limits my movements.

"What's wrong?" Alana's voice is barely audible above the howling wind.

"Something is tracking us."

She goes completely still in my arms. The acrid scent of her fear floods my senses. I lean down and whisper in her ear. "There is a cave not far from here where we may shelter. But, it is high up the cliff face of the mountain. I need you to hold onto my back so I may climb. Are you strong enough to do this?"

"Yes."

"You must hold tight to me. I will have to run."

She lifts her head and nods.

Carefully, she shifts her body. A hiss of pain escapes her as she moves to my back, twining her arms around my neck and her legs around my waist.

I twist my neck back to meet her gaze evenly. "If we are attacked, you must run."

"What about you?"

"Do not worry about me. I will find you."

35

CHAPTER 3

ALANA

His glowing, green eyes search mine, and they look so familiar, I can hardly believe it. "Are you ready?" he asks.

This is the same man from my dreams. I would know him anywhere.

Another howl pierces the silence, ripping me from my thoughts. Fear tightens my chest, but I force myself to push it down. "Ready."

Carefully, he rises from his crouched position, then breaks into a run.

He moves so fast, the landscape blurs all around us. I glance over my shoulder, and movement catches my eye.

Five creatures that look like wolves, but much larger than anything found on Terra, race after us. Their fur is varying shades of brown and gray, standing out against the snow falling heavily and blanketing the ground. Their enormous fangs are bared, their lips curled back in feral snarls as they give chase. Their glowing yellow and orange eyes burn with anger.

Ice cold fear floods my veins. They are like the were-wolves I used to have nightmares about when I was younger.

"Hold on!" Vorek yells.

He leaps through the air toward the rock face. I nearly lose my grip from the sudden stop as he lands against the wall. Vorek scales the mountain with his hands and claws. The powerful muscles of his form moving beneath me as he climbs with dizzying speed.

I watch in horror as the ground falls away below, and the wolves snarl and gnash their teeth as they pursue us up the cliff face.

"They're following us!"

"We are almost there." He grits through his teeth. "You must be quiet. We will have to hide."

My heart pounds as he pulls us up into a cavern. It's so dark in here, I can barely make out anything. The wind howls outside, and the snow falls in thick, heavy sheets, covering Vorek's tracks into the cave as flakes blow into the entrance with each powerful gust of air.

Carefully, he sets me on my feet. His glowing, green eyes meeting mine briefly before he turns back toward the cave mouth.

He stands before me, his feet spread apart in a defensive stance and glances over his shoulder, "Stay behind me."

I do as he says, remaining as still as possible, afraid to even breathe. This cave is large, but my mind fills with the dark memories of my time as a slave. I never used to be claustrophobic, but all the time I spent in a cage has made me fear enclosed spaces.

Gritting my teeth, I force myself to push down this fear and remain still because I know that what hunts us outside is far worse than being in this cave.

We wait for what feels like an eternity before a piercing howl splits the air. Vorek remains tense and unmoving a moment longer before turning back to me. In the darkness of the cavern, the glowing green of his eyes highlights his face just enough that I'm able to make out his features. Despite his impassive expression, it is easy to read the relief in his eyes. "They have gone. We should be safe now."

I open my mouth to speak but stop as he moves to the cave entrance. He taps the wall, and a flicker of light appears in the opening before fading away.

"What was that?"

"A cloaking device. I could not activate it before now or the flash would have drawn their attention. Now that it is in place, it will appear as part of the mountain instead of a cave entrance. It will hide the light of our crystals."

"Our what?"

He moves past me and kneels. I hear something tap together a moment before a soft orange glow fills the space. I glance at his palms and note two large, yellow-orange crystals. He places them atop a small stack in the center of the cave and glances at me. *ᶜL'sair* crystals. Our ship was fortunate to have a large supply when we crashed. We found them on a smuggler's vessel. They should keep the cavern warm tonight."

I allow my gaze to sweep over the cave. The walls are made of dark gray-black rock that looks like stacked slate. It's tall enough near the entrance that, even with his considerable height, Vorek can stand without difficulty. The ceiling slopes down, however, the further you get away from the entrance, and the cavern disappears into darkness.

"How far back does this go?" I ask.

"Not very far," he replies, not exactly answering my question.

Off to one side is what appears to be a sleeping area, piled high with white furs. I notice it's close to the glowing crystals, probably for warmth.

On the opposite side are a stack of four boxes, which I can only assume must be supplies of some sort.

His nostrils flare. "I can still scent your fear. I assure you. We are safe for now. They have gone."

"It's not that," I tell him.

"What is it?"

"I—" I open my mouth to speak, but the words won't come. Closing my eyes, I draw in a deep breath and force them past my lips. "Small and enclosed spaces," I whisper. "I have trouble with them ever since I was kept in cages."

He moves closer, his green eyes full of pain and sadness as they meet mine. "I am sorry, Alana. Truly. If there was anywhere else we could shelter, I would take you. But we do not have a choice."

"It's all right, Vorek." I swallow thickly. "It's something I need to get past anyway, I suppose."

His gaze drops to my torso. "We must treat your wounds."

My fear had made me forget my injuries, but now that he's reminded me, my side begins to throb. He guides me toward the pile of furs.

I bite back a whimper of pain as he helps me to sit.

He removes the bag from his shoulders, and begins rifling through it. He pulls out a tube and holds it up to me. Strange glyphs cover the side and I frown, wondering if he expects me to somehow be able to read it. "This is healing gel. We will use it to mend your injuries."

"What about you?"

"My wounds were not deep. I do not need it."

My mouth drifts open as I study him. I reach out and touch his forearm. His skin now completely closed where jagged claw marks had been less than an hour ago. "How is this possible?" I whisper, more to myself than to him.

He lifts his gaze to mine. "My people heal quickly."

In the glowing light of the crystals, I study his features. He is just as I remember. His hair is short-cropped and raven-black, and his ears have pointed, elvish tips. I scan the sharp lines of his brow and the three slight cranial ridges on his forehead.

As my gaze travels over his aristocratic nose and features, his masculine jaw that could cut glass, and pale skin, his gaze meets mine and I know for sure it is him. I've drawn his face so many times, I would recognize it anywhere. He is just as I've imagined. He is ethereally handsome as he stares down at me.

Kyo told me the V'loryns were known for their lack of emotions, but I don't think he was entirely correct.

Vorek's face is an impassive mask, but it is easy to read the kindness and the emotion behind his glowing green eyes as he studies me in concern.

He holds up the healing gel and examines my wounds. "May I?"

He reaches for me, but I jerk back, hissing in pain at the sudden movement.

Despite his perfect, stoic mask, something akin to sadness flashes behind his eyes. "Please, I want only to help you, Alana. You need not fear me. I would sooner end my own life than ever harm you. My vow."

"I'm sorry. I'm just used to—" I start to say *beatings and shock sticks*, but instead say, "I'm not afraid of you, Vorek. It's just... reflex, I think, after all that I've—" my voice quavers, and I clench my jaw, refusing to break down. "I'm fine."

His expression softens. "You do not need to explain. I cannot imagine what you must have been through."

Dark memories flood my mind. A tear slips down my cheek, but I quickly wipe it away. "Thank you, Vorek."

He reaches for me again, but this time I do not shrink

away. "It will be easier to apply the gel if you lift your clothing."

His cheeks and the tips of his ears flush green as he gestures to my slave dress.

I position one of the furs across my lower body and lift the hem of the paper-thin material to expose the wounds on my torso.

His brow furrows as he studies my injuries. The red slash marks from the A'kai's claws are deep and jagged. "This will be painful, at first, but you must allow it to work."

He spreads some on his hand, and as it hovers over my skin, he flicks his gaze up to mine. "Are you ready?"

Reluctantly, I nod.

He moves closer, and it takes everything inside me not to pull away.

"Wait," I cry out and he jerks his hand back. "How painful is it?"

An almost imperceptible frown creases his brow. "For your species, I do not know. I only know for mine it can be"—he pauses a moment as if searching for the right word before finally deciding—"intense. You must not touch it while it is working. Do you understand?"

I glance down at my wounds, wondering if it wouldn't be better to just let them heal on their own. But, when I shift slightly to prop myself up a bit more, pain arcs across my torso. The red veins spreading out from the nasty claw marks already look like they're harboring infection.

As if sensing my thoughts, he adds. "My people. We are touch telepaths. I can take away some of your pain, if you allow me to open a connection to you."

"Open a connection?"

"A mind link through touch."

"Like the A'kai," I whisper as dark memories begin to creep in.

"Not a violation like that," he quickly says. "It would be a sharing. I could take on some of your pain and help you bear it."

I study him a moment. He is just like in my dreams. Caring and kind. "I… could not ask you to do that," I murmur. "You've already saved me. It wouldn't be right to ask for more."

"I want to help you, Alana," he says, his gaze holding mine. "Please, let me."

I look to the cave entrance and the heavy snowfall outside. Wind howls around the opening, and a small shiver runs through me at the mere thought of how cold it is out there. I remember the ice and snow seemed to stretch out in every direction from the escape pod.

This is an ice world. If I'm going to survive here, I need every advantage I can get. And if this healing gel will close my wounds and stave off infection, that's what I need to do. Vorek is offering to help me with the pain, and I decide to take him up on his offer.

I meet his gaze evenly. "All right."

The moment the gel touches my skin, warmth spreads out from the contact of Vorek's hand on my flesh.

His brow furrows deeply as if in concentration as dull pain centers on my injuries. It's not pleasant, but it's not unbearable either.

I notice the rough edges of my wounds starting to close, the skin reknitting before my very eyes as the healing gel works.

After what feels like an eternity, he removes his hands. I glance down at my torso, and my jaw drops when I notice my perfect skin. Not a single mark remains.

His eyes search mine in concern. "Are you all right?"

"Yes." I sit up, relieved my side no longer hurts. I take his hand and squeeze it gently. "Thank you, Vorek."

His brow furrows deeply as he stares down at our joined hands.

I pull mine away. "Is something wrong?"

"Your species is very... tactile," he says, and I note the hesitation in his tone.

"Is that a bad thing?"

"No," he replies. "I must simply take extra care to maintain my mental transference shields. That is all."

"Mental... transference... shields?"

"We are able to create a barrier—a mental shield—to prevent us from the accidental sharing of thought and emotion through touch. This is how I was able to share your pain but keep our thoughts and emotions separate."

I close my eyes briefly against the painful memory of the A'kai invading my mind.

"I have upset you," he says, and I recognize his statement is also a question.

"The A'kai never cared when they violated my mind. It was the most horrible thing I've ever—" my voice catches and I cannot speak around the sudden knot in my throat.

"The *R'ugol*," he murmurs. "I am sorry they did this to you. I will protect you, Alana. I will take you to my ship and my people. We will keep you safe. My vow."

Even though I have dreamed of him for years, the truth is we've only just met. And yet, when I look in his eyes, I see nothing but truth. He is a good man.

"Are you hungry?" He asks. "Thirsty?"

I nod, and he pulls a nutrient bar from the emergency pack and hands it to me. "Here."

I recognize these. The masters used to give us nutrient bars sometimes when they were feeling generous. They're too hard to chew without softening, so I take the water pack and carefully pour some of the liquid on the bar to soften it.

His brows draw together. "What are you—"

"It's too hard to bite into without softening," I explain.

His gaze drops to my mouth and he frowns. "No fangs," he murmurs.

"What?"

"Your people do not have fangs," he says. "Do you have claws? Venom?"

I shake my head.

His gaze travels over me, considering. "What natural defenses does your species possess?"

"I—" I stop short. I'd never considered this before now. My eyes drift to his nails that I've seen lengthen into deadly claws and I remember how his canines extended into lethal fangs when he fought the A'kai. "My people don't really have any natural defenses."

His mouth drifts open, but he quickly snaps it shut.

I decide to change the subject. "You have a ship?"

"Yes. We crashed here a little over five cycles ago."

"How many of you are there?"

"Including myself, there are seven V'loryns. With the Aerilon, there are seven more." He pauses. "I am uncertain about numbers for the others."

"What others?"

"Ours was not the only ship to crash on this world five cycles ago."

"What happened?"

"We were rendering aid to the Aerilon. Their vessel was damaged near the border with Mosauran space. When they arrived, our communications were down, and we could not respond to their hails. The Mosaurans interpreted our lack of response as a sign of aggression. They fired on us."

My eyes go wide.

He continues. "An A'kai vessel decloaked nearby and the Mosaurans fired on them as well. A Lycaon ship entered into the fray and in the midst of all the fighting, we drifted too close to the wormhole without realizing it. It pulled all of our ships in, and that's how we ended up crashing on this planet."

Worry tightens my chest. "So… there are even more A'kai here than the ones that came down with my people?"

He nods.

"And you said you saw another Terran before you found me?"

"Yes."

"What did she look like?"

His gaze travels down my form and back up to my face. "Similar to you. Small, curved ears. She said her name was Lara."

Hope fills me. "Lara is my friend. Can you take me to her?"

Regret flits briefly across his expression. "She is with the Mosaurans. One of them has claimed her."

"Claimed her? What do you mean?"

"She is his mate."

"His mate?" I inhale sharply as a terrible thought fills my mind. "Did he take her against her will? Is she his slave?"

"Alana, forgive me," he says. "I did not wish to upset you. The Mosaurans may be many things, but slavers they are not. I know this to be truth."

"Then, why would he claim her?"

"I offered her to come with me and my people, but she *chose* to stay with him. She *trusted* him."

"Do you?"

"Commander Markus is an honorable male. Mosaurans believe like my people do—they do not condone slavery. He would not hold her against her will."

"Can you take me to her?"

His features tense, but he dips his head to agree. "First, we must reach my ship. After that, we will go to the Mosauran territory, but we will take more of my people with us."

46

"Why?"

"The Mosaurans, while not our enemies, are not allies, either."

"So... you have an uneasy truce with them?"

"Something to that effect. Yes."

CHAPTER 4

VOREK

A cold breeze whips through the cavern, and she shivers slightly. Her slave dress is paper thin and offers little in the way of warmth or protection. Something about her smaller form and the fact that her people possess no natural defenses calls forth deep and primal possessive instincts inside me.

As I study her face, I am completely fascinated by her luminous blue eyes—a color that is not naturally occurring on our world or our planetary system. She is delicate and lovely. Anger fills me as I think on all she must have suffered. With no way to defend herself, I cannot imagine how terrible her torture must have been.

I remove my tunic and offer it to her, wanting to both keep her warm and cover her with my scent—a primitive way to alert others that she is mine and I will protect and defend her.

She skitters back to the wall.

I freeze at the terrified look on her face. "Forgive me. I

only meant to give this to you to wear... to help keep you warm. Nothing else. I swear it to the goddess."

She gives me a shaky nod, and I hate that she thought I would try to force myself upon her. The mere thought makes bile rise in the back of my throat.

"I'm sorry for my reactions." She lowers her gaze, fighting back tears. "I just—"

"I would never touch you against your will. I swear it to the stars. My vow."

She lifts her eyes to me and extends her arm to take the tunic from my hands. "Thank you." She pauses. "Could you please turn around so I can change?"

I nod and turn my back to her. My pulse pounds in my ears when I hear her slave dress drop to the floor and realize she is standing completely bare behind me. That she trusts me this much, so soon, is humbling to say the least. A soft rustle of clothing follows shortly after.

"You can turn back now."

When I do, my mouth drifts open. The hem of my tunic only goes down to her mid-thigh, and the sleeves are too long; she has rolled them up to her forearms. The neck is so large it hangs off to one side, revealing the bare skin of her left shoulder.

Her long, silken hair hangs over her shoulders in golden waves, an aesthetically pleasing contrast to the slight pink flush of her skin and stunning blue eyes. As she stares up at me, I have suddenly forgotten how to speak, much less form a coherent thought.

Everything about her is both lovely and delicate. But, I know her appearance belies a strength deep inside. She was a prisoner of the A'kai—something known to break most people. Yet, here she stands before me. A survivor in every sense of the word.

Now that she is wearing my shirt, my nostrils flare as I breathe in our combined scent.

Mine.

The word flashes through my mind as my possessive instincts flare even brighter.

I force myself to push this thought aside. She has not agreed to be mine. And even if she did, how would it work between us? We are two different species. My kind have never taken a mate outside of our race. And, yet... the goddess has blessed us with the si'an'inamora—the fated bond.

She turns to the pile of furs and takes half of them, handing them to me.

I push them back in her hands. "No. You need them more than I do."

"I don't want you to be cold, Vorek."

"I will be fine." I'm touched by her concern for me, but given the way she is shivering, I fear if she does not have all of the furs, she could well freeze to death during the night.

She lays down in the nest of furs, and I position myself to keep an eye on both her and the cave entrance during the night. The blizzard is still raging outside, and I doubt the Lycaons will return, but I worry also about the A'kai.

They are much more dangerous than the Lycaons. Because we are so similar in strength and build, it would be more difficult for me to fight them and be certain the outcome would be in my favor.

My gaze drifts to Alana. I cannot bear the thought of her being captured by them again.

"Are you going to sleep?"

"No. I will stay awake and keep watch for a while."

She lowers her head. "Goodnight, Vorek."

"Goodnight, Alana."

She closes her eyes, and I listen to the sound of her

breathing becoming soft and even as she drifts off to sleep. It affords me an opportunity to study her, unobserved.

The light of the l'sair crystals casts her silken hair in a golden glow. Curling my fingers reflexively into my palm, I struggle against the desire to touch her face, ethereal as she sleeps. A softly glowing, white light surrounds her, and I believe it is the si'an'inamora that gives her this glow—a confirmation I have found she who is my Si'an T'kara.

The si'an'inamora is supposed to be a myth. A blessing removed by the gods from my ancestors because of their violent ways. I am the first to find my Si'an T'kara—my fated bondmate—in over two thousand cycles, and the first to find one outside our race.

I wonder if she senses the connection between us.

Unable to sleep, I stand and walk toward the cave entrance. My nostrils flare as I scent the wind, and my eyes scan the storm outside, searching for any sign of danger.

I will die before I allow her to be taken again.

It is concerning that her people do not have any natural defenses, and I wonder how they have managed to survive as a species.

I lower myself to the floor, leaning back against the cave wall near the entrance. I must remain vigilant for any threat to her safety. Even if I were not concerned about the Lycaons and the A'kai, there is still a chance a snowcat could wander too close to our cave and catch her scent.

If I were alone, a predator such as that would probably not bother me, but Alana's scent is… enticingly sweet. Unlike anything I have ever encountered before. At least my tunic masks some of it.

If she were mine, I could mark her as my mate and not have to worry as much that—

Closing my eyes, I force myself to stop this line of thought. She is not mine. Not yet. Until she is, I will be patient. She has been through much. I will not force this bond upon her, nor will I burden her with it, if she does not sense it as I do.

I wish only to take care of her. To shield her and protect her from any and all danger. And even if she never wants me as her mate, I will accept it. I wish only to remain at her side and to help her in any way that I can.

CHAPTER 5

VOREK

loud cry startles me awake. I jerk up to sitting and still, uncertain if I actually heard something.

"No!"

Panic fills me and I race toward Alana to find her thrashing beneath the fur blankets. I drop to my knees beside her and see her eyes are still closed.

She must be having a bad dream.

I make certain my mental shields are intact to prevent accidentally reading her thoughts or emotions, then carefully reach out and place a hand on her shoulder. "Alana?"

Her eyes snap open, wide with fear.

"It's me, Vorek."

"Vorek?" she blinks several times as if coming back to herself.

"You were having a nightmare."

She pulls the furs even tighter around her. Her gaze is locked on the crystals with a faraway look.

"Are you cold?"

She nods absently.

I move to stand, but her small hand on my forearm stops me abruptly. "Thank you, Vorek."

"You are welcome, Alana."

"If you hadn't saved me, I would be dead," she whispers. "The A'kai… they were always drinking from us. They said our blood was special. That it had some sort of restorative properties for them. That's why they are collecting us—Terrans. They are searching for our home world."

My blood runs cold. If the A'kai find her planet, I do not know that they could defend against the might of their evil Empire.

"Where is your world?" I ask. "What planetary system?"

"The Sol system. Do you know it?" she asks.

"No," I reply, and watch the hope leave her eyes with my answer.

She shivers slightly, and I take another l'sair crystal from a container nearby and add it to the hearth to warm her. I look back to find her cocooned beneath the furs, and my heart clenches. I want only to comfort her. "Would you like another nutrient bar?"

"I couldn't possibly eat a whole one."

It worries me how little she has eaten. Her form is slight, and I noticed how easily visible her ribs were earlier when I treated her wound. "What about half?" I ask, hoping to entice her to eat more.

"All right."

I'm pleased she accepts. She is much too thin, and I would see her add some weight to her form to strengthen her health.

We sit side by side near the hearth as she eats her nutrient bar. "My sister and I used to go camping a lot when we were kids."

"Camping?"

"You know, spending the night out in the wilderness. Eating s'mores by a campfire. Sleeping in a tent beneath the stars."

I cock my head to the side. "You are speaking of survival training?"

She laughs, a light and cheerful sound—almost musical and airy in its quality. "No. I mean... just for fun."

I arch a brow.

"You never camped just for fun?"

I shake my head. "When we are children, we are taught survival training. The deserts of my home world can be very unforgiving. It is imperative to learn these skills at a young age. And on the Defense Force, we are given further training on the Moon of—"

"You were in the military?"

"Yes. Rank of Commander."

"A Commander?" She smiles. "That's impressive."

I tip my chin up a bit, glad that she is impressed by my rank.

"I'm a Medical Officer."

"Much more impressive than a Commander," I reply. It is truth. "Healers are invaluable on any ship."

Her smile brightens and I am completely captivated as it lights up her face. "Harry used to tease me that someday I was going to be replaced by a med scanning unit."

"Harry?"

Sadness flits briefly across her expression. "He was on my crew. He and I were the only ones not in stasis sleep when we got taken. The A'kai... they separated us." She blinks back tears. "I saw him before we evacuated the ship, but I don't know if he made it on one of the escape pods."

It is obvious this male is very important to her.

A mate? A lover? Or just a friend?

I want to know, but I cannot bring myself to ask.

She lifts her gaze to me. "We have to find the others, Vorek. Maybe once you get me to Lara, the Mosaurans might help us find them."

Tensing, I nod. Although I dislike the idea of going to the Mosaurans, I will not deny her this, no matter how dangerous it may be. I know for certain they would never harm a female, but what they will do to me and my kin, I am not sure.

We have an uneasy truce between us, but their people are known for their volatile aggression. I will have to pray to the goddess Markus has not forgotten our friendship.

She is silent as she stares into the hearth. I try to think of something to speak of. After a moment, I decide to ask more about her family and home, hoping the reminder of this will help chase away some of the dark memories of her time as a slave. At least for a little while.

"Tell me about your family."

A wistful smile curves her lips. "I have a twin sister, named Amara. She's in the Terran Space Program, too, but she recently took up a post on Mars Station." She sighs. "She fell in love with one of the researchers there, and they're expecting their first child in a few months." She pauses. "At first, I was so jealous of her husband—Jared. I mean... before he came along, it was just the two of us."

I frown as she continues.

"Our parents died when we were younger. So, for a long time, Amara and I only really had each other."

"My soul grieves with yours," I offer her the V'loryn shared words of mourning. I understand loss all too well.

Her eyes brighten with tears, her voice barely a whisper, when she replies, "Thank you. Jared is a good guy. I'm so glad she, at least, has him, now that I'm—" her voice breaks. She draws in a deep breath and blinks back tears. "I've been gone for so long... surely, she's already had the baby by now, and I missed it." She pauses. "I love children. I was so excited when I found out she was expecting," she says wistfully. "I always thought I'd have a family someday."

Children.

I cannot deny I have long desired a mate and family. As I look to her, I wonder if we are even compatible in that way. Then, my thoughts return to Harry, and I sigh heavily. It is on the tip of my tongue to ask if he is her bondmate, but I cannot quite make the words leave my mouth. I am both too fearful and anxious for the answer.

"What about you, Vorek? Do you have any siblings?"

"A younger brother—Tavek. He is here. We both serve on the same ship."

"Your poor parents. I'm sure they must be so worried."

I close my eyes briefly against the pain. "Our parents are gone."

She stares up at me, eyes filled with sadness.

"They perished in the destruction of our home world—V'lorys." I pause, swallowing against the lump in my throat at the painful memory. "My sister—L'yra—and myself and my brother, Tavek, were among the last of the children evacuated to V'lora just prior to our planet's destruction."

"I'm so sorry," she whispers.

"It is not your fault."

"Where is your sister now? Still on V'lora?"

I lower my gaze, pushing down the pain. "She died a few cycles ago before we crashed here. She was taken by slavers, and by the time we found her... it was too late."

"Is that why you saved me?"

I lift my eyes to her. "I saved you because it was the right thing to do. Because I could not stand by and watch an innocent person be abused. Because I—"

"Because you are a good and kind person," her voice

quavers. She takes my hand in hers. I'm surprised by the sudden contact, thankful my mental shields are still in place.

Although it is forbidden to touch one to whom you are not bonded or is not family, I do not pull away. Not from her.

Tears fill her eyes and spill down her cheeks. "I'm sorry. I just... did not expect to find such kindness after all that I've —" Her voice catches.

Gently, I squeeze her hand. "I will do all I can to protect you, Alana. I swear it to the stars. My vow."

"Thank you," she barely manages.

We sit before the light of the hearth a while longer, and she tells me of how she was taken. How she awoke from stasis, found Harry, and was unable to fend off the Anguis who had invaded their ship.

Her story tells me I am right about her as I listen to how she tried to fight off the Anguis to protect her crew. My Si'an T'kara is brave.

"If we make it off this planet, I vow I will do all that I can to help you find your family and your home world again, Alana."

"Thank you."

Her eyelids blink open and closed as she struggles to stay awake. She leans her head against my shoulder, and I still, unsure how to respond.

"You should—" I'm about to tell her she should rest, but when I glance down at her, she is already asleep. Her eyes are closed as she snuggles against me. Carefully, I lift my arm, meaning to help her lay down in the bed, but she nestles into my side.

I wrap my arm around her, tucking the fur tighter around her body to keep her warm, and study her face.

Despite all she had been through, she fought bravely

against her captor, where others might already have broken under the amount of abuse she endured at the hands of the A'kai. She may appear fragile, but she is stronger than she seems.

CHAPTER 6

VOREK

Closing my eyes, I fall away into sleep. Suddenly, I am aware of a faint presence at the edge of my mind. As I study it, myriad emotions rush through me.

Panic, Fear, Concern, Love.

They each rush toward me, crashing against the shore of my mind like waves upon rock, and I realize the onslaught is coming from Alana. But, how is this possible?

"Vorek?" her mind whispers to mine. *"Where are we?"*

Images and flits of memory flow around us like a river, blending together until I am no longer certain which are hers and which are mine. I study them in wonder.

"We are connected in the al'nara—*the mind link."*

Worry fills me. I do not remember forming this connection with her and I am afraid to bring back her terrible memories of the A'kai. Yet, what I sense from her is not fear.

"This is different from that," she whispers in my mind,

having sensed my concern. *"It is not like the A'kai. It is not... forced."*

I quickly create a shared construct to tether her mind as I struggle to understand how it is we are linked in the first place.

We're standing on the balcony of my home, overlooking the city and the sea-green ocean beyond. The yellow sun is bright in the pale-orange sky overhead as the wind carries the crisp, saline scent on the breeze.

"Where are we?"

Her eyes search mine, her long, blonde hair blowing softly around her shoulders. I observe as she gently tucks a few stray tendrils behind the curved shell of her ears.

"My home world. V'lora," I explain. *"This is K'ylira. And in the distance"*—I point toward the sea—*"is the castle of House D'enekai and the ocean beyond."*

She leans down and picks one of the glowing, purple flowers from the thick, green vines climbing up the exterior walls of my home. She brings it to her nose and inhales deeply, smiling. *"It feels so real. I can even smell the flowers."*

Concentrating, I change the construct so we are standing in the middle of the city gardens. Lush, green grass covers the entire space. We walk along the gravel pathway, following one of the nearby streams winding under and beside it. Various trees and flowering plants with bright purple, yellow, and red blossoms line the walkway.

A *ritak* crosses our path with a litter of seven, each of their fluffy, little, white bodies toddling after their mother. Alana kneels to pet it. *"A ritak,"* she murmurs, having read my mind to search for what it is.

The creature begins to emit a low purr.

She laughs and warmth blooms in my chest, spreading throughout my entire body. I have never felt anything like this.

"Is this what you feel when you experience joy?"

"Yes." She takes my hand. *"Your home world is beautiful."*

Beautiful. This word whispers through my mind. There is no equivalent in the V'loryn tongue, but I find it is the only word that can accurately describe Alana.

Sadness tightens my chest. *"The gardens were made to remind us of our world that was lost—V'lorys-that-was."*

I focus, and then we are standing in the desert. "This is the natural landscape of V'lora," I murmur.

Wisps of dust and mica sweep across the dunes as we gaze out at the red sands. A large shadow passes overhead, and she lifts her gaze, her jaw dropping as her eyes widen. *"Dragons,"* she whispers. *"You have real* dragons."

The large *v'rach* spreads its wings wide as it sails along the current. *"V'rachs,"* I correct.

A woman in the distance catches her eye, and my breath hitches as I recognize what my mind has brought to the surface—her long, black hair intricately braided and hanging down one shoulder, her glowing, green eyes observing us with a softened expression.

I blink, and she is gone.

"Who was that?"

"My sister—L'yra."

Sadness and despair wash over and through me. I had not meant to show her this, but I realize *we* are not supposed to be here, either. The *al'nara* is sacred—an act only meant to be shared between bondmates.

Guilt and shame fill me as Alana's eyes brighten with tears. *"Forgive me. I should not have brought you here."*

CHAPTER 7

ALANA

As my mind slowly comes back into awareness, I'm snuggled against something warm. The soft scent of cinnamon and spice fills my nostrils, and I breathe it in deep, stretching beneath the warm comforter.

My eyes snap open when I remember where I am. I lift my head and find Vorek staring back at me. Suddenly embarrassed, I quickly push away from him. "I-I'm sorry. I didn't mean to—"

The memory of my dream resurfaces, and I frown at recalling the lucid and vivid nature of it. Although I have dreamed of him many times, this time was different. I study Vorek. "Was that... real?"

Despite his impassive expression, guilt is easily read behind his eyes. "Yes. Forgive me. I... my mental shields must have been lowered as I slept. When you touched me, it created a telepathic connection between us—the *al'nara*."

Tears sting my eyes at the haunting memory of the woman in the desert. "Your sister... I'm so sorry, Vorek."

He swallows thickly and lowers his gaze. "Thank you."

"I had heard your people do not have emotions." The echoes of the intense pain and sadness I felt from him in the al'nara still lingers in my mind. "But you *do* feel, don't you?"

He lifts his gaze to mine and, although he is V'loryn, the pain is easily read in his features. "Yes, we do. We are taught to suppress emotion from a young age. As a result, we have… difficulty processing and understanding them. It is part of our culture to place rational thought over emotion, in all things."

"Why?"

"The Ancient Ones were much more expressive of their emotions than we are now. In their violent ambition to expand our Empire, they tried to create a race of master soldiers that would be unhindered by emotional constraints. They developed a procedure that targeted the emotional center of the brain.

"Instead of creating superior warriors, it led to a golden age of peace and reason. Although this treatment has not been used in over one thousand cycles, every V'loryn is taught emotional suppression to ensure our society remains on this path."

His grief over his sister was an overwhelming ocean of despair. I understand this because I experienced it, too, with the loss of my parents.

I open my mouth to say something else, but he quickly changes the subject, darting a glance at the cave entrance. "The storm is still raging outside. It is not safe to leave yet. But, as soon as it abates, we should go quickly."

"Why?"

"I fear the Lycaons will return to search for us."

His answer fills me with dread. The last thing I want is to be hunted down by werewolves.

"How far is it to your people from here?"

"Less than a day's travel."

I look down at my tattered shoes which are little more than slip-ons, at best. Vorek's gaze follows my line of sight. "We can cover your feet with some of the fur hides." He kneels and lifts his gaze to mine. "May I?"

I nod, and he grabs one of the fur blankets and brings it to my foot, measuring. I love that he doesn't just touch me without asking. When I was a slave, I had no control over anything to do with my body. The fact that he not only recognizes this, but respects my boundaries, means so much to me.

Carefully, he lifts my foot, his brow furrowing in a contemplative look. "What is it?" I ask, curious about his expression.

"Your feet. They are so small."

"Small?" I laugh, wiggling my toes. "My feet are average size."

He arches a brow but says nothing. Then, he lifts his hand, and my mouth drifts open as his nails extend into sharpened claws. I watch him begin slicing through the leather hide as if it were little more than tissue paper.

His eyes snap up to mine, and he quickly retracts them. "Forgive me," he says quickly. "I did not mean to scare you."

I hate the pain in his eyes at the thought that I would fear him, so I quickly move to reassure him. "I'm not afraid of you, Vorek. After all, if you wanted to hurt me, you could have done so over a dozen times by now."

His green eyes meet mine evenly. "I would never harm you, Alana."

"I know." I give him a warm smile. "That's why I trust you."

He blinks several times to regard me, then bows his head low. "I am honored by your trust. I vow never to break it."

I observe as he goes about covering my feet. He's very

methodical in his measurements and cuts. He slices a line down the fabric to make a piece of twine he uses to sew the pieces of fur together. He takes a few more of the pelts and cuts a hole for my head to layer them over the tunic he gave me, for extra warmth. When he's finished, my body and feet are warm. Even though the coverings have no hard soles, I feel much better about walking in these than I do with my slave shoes.

A low howl sounds in the distance, and my heart starts thundering in my chest. I look to Vorek. "Do you think they're searching for us again?"

The wind whips around the cave outside as the heavy snowfall continues, obscuring my view of anything beyond the cavern entrance.

"No. They are simply reminding us they are nearby. As soon as the storm weakens a bit, we must be ready to leave." He pulls the blaster from his belt and holds it out to me. "Do you know how to use this?"

"I've been trained with weapons, but not this particular type. I'm a good aim, though."

I take it from him, and he begins to explain the various buttons and settings, then he frowns. "It appears only the stun setting still works. It must have been damaged somehow. Perhaps, during the crash." He lifts his gaze to me. "We will practice."

"Where?"

He moves across the cave and places a stone near the far wall. "Aim for this. If you miss, it will only hit rock."

He stands off to my side as I raise the blaster and take careful aim. Depressing the button, I miss the target entirely and release a heavy sigh of frustration. "How do I aim this?"

Vorek cocks his head to the side and gestures to the blaster. "May I?"

I nod, and he moves behind me, reaching his arms around

my form and placing his hands over mine on the blaster. His breath is warm in my ear as he whispers. "Line it up like so." His grip tightens just enough to raise the blaster a bit.

My cheeks flare with heat, and my heart beats a frantic rhythm in my chest. His body is almost completely enveloping mine, the warm cinnamon and spice of his scent surrounding me. When he whispers in my ear again, I draw in a shaking breath, my entire body humming in awareness of him. "Now, you will line up these two sights, and it should be square on the target."

I nod and depress the trigger, hitting it directly in the center. The small char mark proving my aim was true.

I turn to him and smile, but then inhale sharply. His face is so close to my own, the warmth of his breath fans across my lips. His glowing, green gaze holds mine and something —an emotion—flashes briefly behind his eyes, but it's gone too quickly for me to know what it is. He steps back, and his lips quirk up ever so slightly at the edges. "Well done."

I fire a few more practice shots before I'm satisfied I have it down and turn to him. "I fought the A'kai before you came. Several times, but he always bested me." He says nothing, so I continue. "Show me your fighting techniques so I can incor-porate them into—"

"No," he replies, cutting me off abruptly.

I blink at him, surprised by his answer. "Why not?"

"Because I do not wish to harm you."

I shake my head. "If you teach me, you can be careful and—"

"You are much smaller than me. I will not risk hurting you."

"I need to be able to defend myself," I counter.

"*I* will defend you," he states firmly.

"And what if you fail?"

He clenches his jaw as he lowers his gaze, considering.

71

When he tips his head back up to mine, it is easy to read the worry in his eyes. "I will show you the defensive holds, but that is all. I... cannot risk accidentally harming you, Alana."

It's on the tip of my tongue to protest, but I don't. My gaze drifts to the outside and the storm raging beyond the cave mouth. We don't have time to be arguing.

At least, he's going to teach me something. I can argue for the rest later.

"Good. Show me the holds."

As we go through the various poses, he is impressed by how quickly I am able to break free. However, the last one, he assures, will not be so easy.

He moves behind me and bands one strong arm around my waist, pulling me back against the solid wall of his chest, while his other wraps around my upper body, his hand cupping my jaw and neck. Completely immobilized, with my arms at my sides and chin tipped up, exposing my neck, he leans down and whispers in my ear. "Show me how you would break free of this."

My entire body flushes with warmth. We're so close, there is no space between our bodies. In this position, I can feel his heart beating in his chest, against my back. I twist my neck just enough to look back at him.

We've only just met, but I've dreamed of him for so many years it feels as if I've known him forever. As my gaze travels over his face, I recall all the times I drew him from memory. None of my drawings ever truly captured just how handsome he is.

He wants me to break free, but my gaze drops to his lips, and I'm already imagining what it would be like to stretch up on my toes just enough to press my mouth to his.

I used to dream of this many times. My grandmother said my mother dreamed of my father before they met.

Softly shaking my head, I force myself to focus. I hardly

know Vorek. I doubt he even finds me attractive. Besides, we are two different species. But as his eyes meet mine, I realize how easy it would be to lose myself in them.

After all the years I've dreamed of this man, I'm already half-way in love with him. He doesn't know it, but my dreams of him are the reason I survived. They are what kept me going when it would have been easier to simply give up.

As his gaze holds mine and the silence stretches between us, I wonder if perhaps my desire may not be entirely one-sided.

CHAPTER 8

VOREK

Her luminous eyes search mine a moment before her gaze drops to my mouth. Holding her so close like this, my heart pounds in my chest. My nostrils flare as her delicate scent grows stronger, and my *l'ok* begins to lengthen and extend, hardening painfully with want to join my body to hers.

She turns just enough that her lips brush softly against mine. I draw in a shaking breath at the delicate touch as need burns through me like fire.

I quickly drop my arms and move away from her, not wanting to scare her with my body's reactions to her nearness. She has been through much, and I do not want her to be afraid of me.

"I'm sorry," she says. "I shouldn't have—"

"Forgive me," I cut her off. "My body was reacting to your nearness. I… did not want you to fear me. I would never touch you against your will. My vow."

Her small brow furrows. "Your body was—" she stops

abruptly, dawned understanding spreading across her features. She blinks several times. "Are you saying you're attracted to me?"

My gaze holds hers. "Yes."

We stare at each other in silence and I'm unable to speak.

Drawing in a deep breath, I open my mouth to reply, but another howl fills the air, this one much closer than the last. I whip my head in the direction of the cave entrance, and my nostrils flare at the scent of a Lycaon nearby.

I turn back to her. "We must leave."

"But, the storm—"

"We must risk it. They are here."

The acrid scent of her fear fills the air.

"You must hold onto me like before so I can climb down the mountain."

Using a piece of twine I cut as a belt, I quickly smooth out her fur coverings and tighten it over them, tucking the blaster inside. I turn and kneel so she can climb onto my back. She wraps her arms around my neck and her legs tightly around my waist.

"Are you ready?" I ask over my shoulder.

"Yes."

Without hesitation, I race out of the cave. Lengthening my nails into claws, I dig them deep into the cliff face as I scale down the wall.

The hair rises on the back of my neck as a string of howls fills the air.

The pack knows we are here. I must hurry.

Alana holds tightly to me as we descend. Another howl rings out, and she shivers slightly. My protective instincts flare, something dark and primal unfurling from deep inside me.

I will tear apart anyone who dares to try and harm her. She is mine, and I will allow no one to take her from me.

The icy wind pulls at my form, trying to rip me away from the cliff wall, but I hold fast, tumbling bits of rock and snow falling from overhead. Looking up to the top, my heart pounds when I notice one of the Lycaons not far above us. His vision is not as sharp as mine, however, and he does not realize how close we are as his eyes search through the heavy snowfall.

I scent another one nearby and carefully position us between two large boulders jutting out from the wall, shielding us a bit from the wind and, hopefully, the Lycaon's sight.

I pull Alana around to my front and press her back into the wall in an attempt to hide us behind the large rocks. Her heart pounds in her chest against mine. "Vorek," she whispers against me. "I'm slowing you down. You have to leave me behind."

"No. I will not."

"But, I—"

"I will not leave you here, Alana. Hold tightly to me. I have a plan."

She goes silent, and her legs and arms tighten around my form.

Looking over my shoulder, I observe the drop is not far from here to the ground. "I am going to jump."

She lifts her head to look down. "We can't, Vorek. It's too far."

I meet her gaze evenly. "Do you trust me?"

"Yes."

My heart soars as she answers without hesitation. "Then, hold on."

I push away from the cliff wall and wrap my arms firmly around her smaller frame for our descent to the ground below.

CHAPTER 9

ALANA

My heart slams in my throat as Vorek pushes off of the wall, and we begin falling toward the ground with dizzying speed.

The breath escapes my lungs in a sudden rush as his feet hit the earth. I don't even have time to catch my breath before he begins running so fast the forest around us is a blur of trees.

Something crashes through the woods behind us, and I squint my eyes through the falling snow and realize it's the wolves. Holding tight to Vorek with my legs and one arm, I use my free hand to pull the blaster from my belt.

I aim over Vorek's shoulder at the Lycaon and depress the button. Light arcs from the barrel and races toward the wolf, hitting him square in the chest. Instantly stunned, he drops like a stone to the ground.

My triumph is short-lived, however, when I see four more still behind us. They howl their rage as they chase after us. I fire again, but miss, as they dodge to one side before my shot finds its mark.

"There are too many of them," I tell Vorek as I try to aim at another and miss.

"Hold tightly to me," Vorek says urgently in my ear. "This next part will be dangerous."

I quickly tuck the blaster back in my belt and wrap both arms around his neck. My mind spins as I conjure all sorts of terrifying things, wondering what could possibly be more dangerous than literally jumping off a cliff wall and being chased by wolves.

Terror lodges in my throat as the dull roar of water sounds up ahead. "What are you going to do?"

"If we can make it across, they will not follow."

I open my mouth to protest that I could freeze if we fall in the icy water, but I don't. As the Lycaons gain on us, I realize we have no other choice.

We'll either make it or we won't, but I will not be anyone's slave. Never again.

CHAPTER 10

VOREK

I wrap my arms tightly around her as we race through the forest. I will die, or I will save her, but I will not allow her to be captured by the A'kai or the Lycaons.

The Lycaons are an extremely territorial species and have been pushing the boundaries of their area farther and farther each cycle. We have maintained an uneasy truce with them thus far, but I am questioning the logic of this decision. Especially given the burden I carry now.

I do not want her to fall into their hands. They are almost as savage as the A'kai. Even the Mosaurans, for all their volatile aggression and warrior culture, are more civilized than them.

The Lycaons are one of the only species that can move as fast as mine, but we are much stronger. If I were alone, I would not be so concerned, but with Alana, I cannot risk being caught out in the open. I would be unable to defend both myself and her, if I had to fight off their pack.

"How many are behind us?"

"I stunned one, but there are still four."

At last count, I knew there were at least seven of them. Lycaons are known for hunting in packs.

The deafening roar of blood in my ears drowns out all other noise, save for the high-pitched howls echoing through the woods. They are trying to confuse and surround us, but we will not become their prey.

They are too close for us to make it to the mountain pass and to the ship beyond. We need somewhere to hide. But, first, I must find a way to make them lose our trail.

A thought occurs to me, but it is dangerous. As I glance at my Si'an T'kara in my arms, I know I do not have a choice. I will not allow her to escape one captor only to be taken by another.

I make a sharp turn through the trees and head out toward the river. It is wide and deep, but there is a way to cross. I discovered it a few cycles ago, when I was out hunting. It is fed by a warm spring so the water is not ice-cold, but it is not exactly warm either.

The Lycaons used to pass this way, but no more. Not after they nearly lost one of their own when he pursued me across this dangerous path.

As I break through the woods and out into the clearing, the dull roar of the water ahead fills me with hope.

If I can make it across with Alana in time, the Lycaons will not follow.

This part of the river is less than an *arcum* from the falls. Sharp rocks jut up from the riverbed as the current flows roughly around them, spilling over the edge into the forest below.

Alana's legs and arms tighten around me, and I hold just as tightly to her, afraid she might fall. If she can barely tolerate cold weather when she is dry, I fear that even despite the warm spring that feeds it, if she were to fall into the river, she could become hypothermic.

Without hesitation, I jump from the shore onto the closest rock. Picking my way across, I am careful to choose only the stones that have ample footing.

Clenching my jaw, I force myself to remain focused as the howls grow louder behind me, the Lycaons voicing their anger and frustration that I am getting away. I dare not look back to see how many wait on the river's bank, but I know they are many, for I can scent the stench of their fur on the breeze.

"Give us the female!" one of them calls out, and I recognize Luken's voice straight away.

As their alpha, I understand he speaks for the rest of the pack. I do not doubt he has many of his males with him, and I would be foolish to try to stand and face them now.

"No!" I reply, not bothering to look back for fear I may slip and fall away into the water. "You cannot have her!"

"I will not let you take her, V'loryn," Luken growls, his voice much too close behind me for my liking.

A sharp scrape of claws against stone makes the hair rise on my neck.

"He's close," Alana's voice is panicked in my ear.

She reaches for the blaster just as I jump to the next stone. It fumbles from her hands and splashes into the water. "No," she breathes out.

I want to reassure her it is all right. That I will get us across and we will be safe on the other side, but I cannot speak. It is taking all my concentration to move from one stone to the next.

My people do not swim. The gravity on our home world is greater than most others. Our increased body density, as a result of this, makes it nearly impossible to remain above water without great effort. I cannot afford to fall. If I did, it could be fatal for both of us.

Alana cries out a moment before sharp pain rips across my back. The claws of the Lycaon tearing through my flesh.

Stumbling forward, I lose my footing, falling into the icy depths below.

The strong current rips her from my arms as we go tumbling through the water. My feet scrape along the riverbed. It's shallow enough I'm able to push myself up, gasping for air as we're pulled along.

Alana wraps one arm around a rock nearby. She reaches for me, and I take her hand.

But, I am too heavy, and her grip on the rock begins to slip as she tries to hold onto me. "I am too heavy," I tell her as I release her hand. "You must let me go."

"No," she cries out, refusing to let go of my wrist. "I won't."

I open my mouth to argue, but a heavy log hits the side of my body, making the decision for us both, dragging me away from her. I hold tightly to the log, barely able to keep my head above water as the current drags and swirls around several rocks, threatening to pull me under the closer I get to the waterfall's edge.

"Vorek!" Alana cries out. I watch in horror as she loses her grip, and the water takes her, dragging her toward me.

She reaches for me, and I reach back, taking her smaller hand in mine. Desperate to save her, I try to push her toward the shore, but the current is too strong.

"Vorek!" she yells, her eyes wide as she looks over my shoulder.

I follow her line of sight and panic wraps tight around my spine as we rush toward the falls.

I turn back to her. Her eyes meet mine and the world

shifts into slow motion as, together, we drop over the edge, tumbling away in the roaring falls.

Curling myself protectively around her smaller form, I tuck her close to my chest, wanting to shield her with my body from any sharp rocks below.

My back hits the water, and it swallows us both. Pain shoots through my left arm and leg as I scrape against a giant boulder as the violent current drags us downstream. We are near the riverbank. It's shallow enough here I can push myself up just enough to draw in deep gulping breaths of air before my dense body weight pulls me back down beneath the water.

I wrap my hands around Alana's waist to push her up and away, but she holds fast to me as we are pulled into deeper water.

She floats to the surface, still holding onto my arm, and then pulls herself back down to me.

Desperate for air, my lungs burn at the struggle to hold my breath, the desire to inhale threatening to overwhelm me. As my oxygen begins to deplete, my emotions break to the surface. I touch her face, opening a mental connection between us as I speak in her mind. *"You must let me go, or you will drown."*

"No. I'm going to save you."

Emotions overwhelm and move through me. *"You must let me go so you may live, my Si'an T'kara."*

Before I can say anything else, she pulls herself toward me. *"I won't let you die, Vorek,"* she whispers in my mind. Our eyes lock a moment before she presses her lips to mine, sealing her mouth over my own and breathing air into my starving lungs, giving me strength.

"I'm going to push you toward the shore."

Before she can protest, I push her toward the riverbank and watch as she disappears above the water's surface.

Using the last of my strength, I grip a nearby rock jutting up from the riverbed and use it to push myself toward the shallows until I'm able to gain my footing and drag myself onto the shore.

Exhausted, I crawl onto the sand and collapse onto my back, panting heavily as I stare up at the blue-gray sky and the dark clouds overhead.

Alana collapses beside me, her knees pulled to her chest, shivering. "Vorek," she barely manages through chattering teeth. "Are you all right?"

A sharp howl in the distance draws my attention. My focus shifts back to the river to see the silhouettes of the Lycaons at the top of the falls, searching for a way down to us. It is only a matter of time.

Gathering my strength, I manage to sit up. I pull Alana into my arms and tuck her close to my chest. Her entire body is trembling from the cold. I have to find shelter. Someway to get her warm.

Our emergency supply pack is gone, swept away by the current, and we no longer have the blaster, either.

Exhausted, I force myself to put one foot in front of the other and stagger toward the tree line.

Snow blankets the area around us as I make my way toward the nearest tree. I fall to my knees, careful to lay Alana down gently beside me. She stares up at me in concern and takes my hand. "I'm sorry, Vorek. I can walk, I just need a moment to—" her voice stops as her shivering grows worse.

"I need energy," I tell her. "I must use the Balance before I can go any further."

"The what?"

"The Balance."

The Lycaons howl again, and I know I do not have time to explain. Placing my palm on the dark-gray trunk, I bow my head in concentration as I reach for the pulsing energy of the tree.

Primal energy courses through my veins as I draw from the tree's lifeforce. I have only ever done this once before, and it is as hard now as it was then. It takes everything within me to focus on taking only what I need and no more.

The pulsing lifeforce of the tree flows into my own, strengthening me. Warmth floods my veins as the energy courses through my body. It is tempting to keep drawing from the tree, but I force myself to pull back. I do not want to kill it.

My eyes flash open, and I remove my hand, standing with renewed vigor and determination. My injuries are now healed, and all traces of fatigue have left me.

I pull Alana into my arms and notice her staring at the tree. Her mouth is agape as her gaze travels over the branches and leaves that are now drooping after I took from them to replenish myself.

"What did you do?" her voice is barely a whisper.

"I will explain later. We have to go."

I turn and race along the river. We must find a place to hide, somewhere the Lycaons cannot scent us. The terrible shivering of Alana's form worries me. I must get her somewhere I can warm her, or else, I worry she will not make it through the night.

My ship is still too far away, and I know, without checking, there is no signal on my wrist comm here. We are not close enough to reach anyone. Not yet.

The Lycaon's howls grow closer as I race along the riverbank. Another waterfall lies up ahead, and I glance down at my Si'an T'kara. "Alana?"

She barely manages to lift her head.

"I need you to hold onto me. Like you did when we climbed down the mountain. Can you do that?"

She nods, and I turn her in my arms so her legs wrap around my waist, her arms around my neck. As I approach the edge, I carefully look over.

It is not as far a drop as the other falls, but far enough I will have to climb down. I cannot risk jumping from this height. If I were alone, I might risk it, but I cannot take a chance with Alana. She could be hurt, and I would never be able to live with myself if any harm came to her.

Cautiously, I drop over the side and begin the descent. Her grip is not as tight on me as I would like, but I cannot hold onto her and climb at the same time. "You must not let go," I tell her. "We are almost to the bottom."

She nods against my chest, unable to speak through her shivering.

As I climb down, heat radiates onto my palms from the rock wall. There are many warm springs on this planet, and I suspect the warmth comes from one nearby. I follow it to the areas that are warmer and notice a small opening.

It is just big enough to squeeze through and get behind the water curtain of the falls.

I send a silent prayer to the goddess when it opens into a large cave. The walls are even warmer here when I place my hand upon them, and as my eyes pierce the darkness, I observe a fine mist of steam rising from a small pool near the back. I walk toward it and carefully lay Alana down on the heated, stone floor.

The air is still cold, but this is much better than being outside, by far. I cup her chin and tip her face up to me. "Alana, we need to remove your wet clothes."

Weakly, she nods. I help her pull the sopping wet furs from her body. When we get down to her slave dress, a piercing howl echoes from outside. I meet her gaze evenly. "This cave has a warm spring. The floor has enough heat to warm you until I get back."

I tear a strip from one of her fur coverings that carries her scent. I stand, meaning to leave, but her small hand on my forearm stops me abruptly. "Where are you going?"

"I must lead the Lycaons away from here. I will circle back after I have lost them and return as soon as I can."

"Don't go," she whispers. "It's too dangerous. You could be hurt."

My heart clenches at her concern. I place my hand atop hers, on my arm, squeezing it gently. "I will be fine. And I promise, I will return to you quickly, my Si'an T'kara. My vow."

"Si'an T'kara," she whispers, her small brow furrowed. "I've heard this before, in my dreams."

I want to ask her what she means, but there isn't time. I spin toward the cave entrance.

"Vorek, wait!" she calls, but I leave before she can say anything else, and I dare not look back. I do not have time. My nostrils flare as I scent the Lycaons. They are nearby—much too close for my liking. I have to lead them away.

I slip out from behind the curtain of water and jump the rest of the way down, landing on my feet at the base of the falls. Without hesitation, I break into a run, racing away as fast as I can.

I cannot afford for the Lycaons to see me. If they do, they will know I no longer have Alana with me and will figure out I am trying to lead them away from her.

A chorus of howls, and the sounds of pursuit, chase after me as I race along the riverbanks and then turn to rush into the forest. My footsteps in the snow will leave an easy trail for them to follow.

As I run past several trees, I make sure to allow Alana's fur cloak to brush against them, marking a trail with her scent, so they believe she is with me. Snow falls heavily around me as I sprint through the forest.

This is good. If the weather remains like this, it will help cover my tracks for the return journey to the cave.

A cold wind blows through the woods, carrying the scent of at least six distinct Lycaons. Their foul stench seeming to come from several different directions. They are pack hunters, skilled in guiding their quarry where they wish. They are trying to flank me and herd me into an ambush.

I grit my teeth in determination. The Lycaon are used to dealing with lesser creatures, not something sentient that can anticipate their trap. My heart pounds as I think on Alana. I will not be caught, and I will not fail her.

I hasten back to the river. Several large rocks jut up from the surface, a reflective coating of ice along the tops making them treacherous, but I must risk crossing. If I slip and fall into the water, I could drown, but I do not have a choice. It is the only way to lose the Lycaons and return to Alana.

As I study the turbulent water, another thought occurs to me. Before I cross, I must give the Lycaons something else to chase besides me. I break off two branches the width of my wrist from the closest tree. Bringing the strip of Alana's fur covering to my body, I press it to my chest to transfer my scent. I wrap it around the two branches and tie them together.

Carefully, I set it in the water and push it away, watching as it floats downstream. The current is strong and fast, and should carry this distraction rather far before they catch up to it.

Turning my attention back to the river, I take the first step onto the rocks. My heart hammers as I cautiously pick my way across, careful in my footing. I am only three steps away from the opposite bank. I jump to the next rock, and my foot hits a patch of ice; I slip, plunging into the icy water.

The air explodes from my lungs as the current slams me into a boulder beneath the surface. Gripping it tightly, I struggle against the strong torrent trying to rip me away. If I let go, I will be lost.

Thoughts of Alana fill my mind as I imagine her alone in the cavern waiting for me.

I have to get back to her.

The A'kai and the Lycaons are hunting her. I cannot fail her.

Renewed determination fills me, and I use all of my strength to fight the violent current, pulling myself out of the turbulent water. I grab the closest rock and drag myself closer to shore.

The river is cold as ice, but I remain waist deep as I wade upstream, hiding myself behind large rock formations as I go. A noise in the distance draws my attention, and I crouch low, peering over one of the boulders.

On the opposite bank the Lycaon pack tracks the shoreline, their nostrils flaring as they lift their heads to scent the air. They are still in their four-legged form, making their way along the river. One of them stops, and the rest go still, as if waiting for his command.

Even in his beastly form, I recognize Luken. He is their Alpha. His glowing, orange eyes sweep out over the water, as though he senses me nearby.

I shut my eyes tight, not wanting the glowing green color to give me away in the near darkness. My pulse pounds in my ears. If they find me, I will have no choice but to run farther downstream, leading them away from my Si'an T'kara.

I cannot allow them to return to the cavern and discover Alana.

I send a silent prayer to the goddess. If I have to run, I do not know when I will be able to get back to her. I hate the idea of leaving her for so long, all alone. Anything could happen while I am gone. She could freeze, or even be discovered by a predator—a snowcat, or something much worse.

The Lycaons and the A'kai are not the only creatures to hunt in the ice and snow on this world.

The Lycaon gives a low, keening howl, followed by the sounds of their paws crunching through the snowy landscape as they continue downstream, following the false scent trail I have left them.

My heart hammers as I wait a few moments more, praying they do not suspect my deception. I train my ears, listening for any sounds of their return. After what feels like forever, I wade out of the water toward the shoreline.

Without hesitation, I break into a run, charging back toward the falls and the cavern, praying my Si'an T'kara is all right.

CHAPTER 11

ALANA

"Vorek, don't go!" I call out, but he disappears before I can stop him.

Shivering and cold, I somehow manage to right myself. My limbs are heavy and shaking, but I force myself toward the cavern entrance, hoping to catch him before he leaves.

The roar of the falls muffles the loud howls sounding in the distance, so I cannot tell how close they are. But, it doesn't matter. The fact that I can hear them at all means I'm too late.

Vorek cannot turn back. Not now. They'd surely catch him. I can do nothing but wait—wait and pray he returns safely.

The cavern is warm, but it isn't enough to stop me from shivering. I make my way toward the back of the cave, running my hand along the wall's rough surface to guide my steps. Night has fallen outside and I'm thankful the moon is full, providing enough illumination that I can still see the cavern entrance when I glance over my shoulder.

It's enough to give me confidence to continue toward the warm springs despite how dark it is as I continue toward the back.

The stone floor grows warmer and a fine mist of steam hovers in the air as I approach the pool near the back of the cave.

My feet bump into something soft, and I realize it's the pile of my sopping wet furs. I kneel and carefully spread them out along the floor so the heat will dry them.

The sound of dripping water echoes softly throughout the space, and I continue my exploration to find the pool. Placing one foot in front of the other, with my hand tracing along the wall, I advance deeper. The steam rising up from the floor thickens around me, surrounding me with warmth. I carefully sweep my foot out, and find the edge of the water.

It's so dark back here, I can barely see my hand in front of my face. Dropping to my knees near the edge. I start to remove my slave dress, but I hate the idea of being completely nude. Especially since I don't know when I might need to run or fight.

My hands trace along the threadbare material, and a thought occurs to me. I no longer need this dress, and it already provides very little in the way of warmth.

I grip the hem and pull it over my head. Laying it down on the floor before me, I measure, first the span of two, then four hand widths. Carefully, I tear the two long strips, the material giving way easily.

I wrap the smaller portion and tie it around my breasts, the other, I tie around my hips like a short skirt. I'm still wet, but it's not nearly as bad as when I was completely covered.

I submerge myself in the water and a small sigh of contentment escapes my lips. I don't allow myself to remain very long, however, because I need to be ready to run when Vorek returns. If he cannot lose the Lycaons, we'll have to find somewhere else to shelter.

I lie down on the heated flooring and curl into a ball on my side. It's not exactly comfortable, but it's better than nothing. At least there is heat back here, so I no longer feel so cold. As I wait for Vorek to return. I pray nothing has happened to him.

If he doesn't come back soon, I'm going to search for him.

I'm not entirely helpless. I've had survival training. And I know I'm on an alien planet, but I have to try, if he doesn't return soon. I know he'd do the same for me. He's already proven that several times. I would be dead by now if not for him.

Sighing heavily, I think on my dreams. I've never been one to believe in fate, but it cannot be coincidence that I dreamed of him for the past five years. He is exactly as I remember.

Si'an T'kara. I think back on the words he said before he left. He called me this in my dreams, but I don't know what it means.

His people may appear similar to the A'kai, but they are as different as night and day. Closing my eyes, I can still picture his face when he vowed he would protect me. Part of me wonders if he might somehow recognize me too. Maybe he has dreamed of me as well.

Despite his impassive expression, I can easily read the emotions behind his eyes. When he made his vow to take care of me, he meant it. After all I've been through, I had forgotten that such kindness could still exist in the universe.

But, it's more than that. There's something about him that draws me in. It certainly doesn't hurt that he's devastatingly handsome. Even as I think this, I recognize that now is not an ideal time to be attracted to someone. Our lives are in danger and we're being hunted. Yet, I can't help but feel that this is something else. Something deeper. As if my soul somehow recognizes his in some strange way.

When my grandmother told me of how my mother dreamed of my father, before they met, I didn't entirely believe her. I thought it was just some romantic story she told me to try to somehow dull the terrible pain of their passing. But now... I'm not so sure.

The sound of dripping water is quickly followed by a scraping noise along the stone. I go still, my eyes searching the darkness for any movement.

Glowing, green eyes blink at me, and I inhale sharply. My heart pounds in my chest as I jerk up to my feet. "Vorek, is that you?"

"You do not recognize me?"

I frown. "There's hardly any light in here. I can only see your eyes."

"Your species cannot see in the dark?"

"No. Can yours?"

"Yes."

Suddenly, self-conscious of what I'm wearing, my cheeks heat in embarrassment, because I know this material is paper thin, hiding nothing when wet.

A sudden rush of air buffets my body, and I blink in shock as Vorek's green eyes are mere centimeters from my face. This close, their glow casts just enough light that I can make out his features.

His brow furrows deeply. "Are you ill?"

"What?"

"You are shivering, and your skin... it is red, now, across your cheeks."

"I'm just... cold," I reply, my teeth chattering slightly, despite my trying to speak evenly.

This near, I can feel the warmth of his body radiating to

mine. He wraps his arms around me, and I breathe out a long exhale. "You're so warm." I snuggle into him, pressing my cheek against the hard planes of muscle lining his bare chest.

He stills, and so do I as I recall his comment about how "tactile" my species is. I lift my eyes to his. "Is this... all right?"

He nods then guides me to the near wall, and we sit on the floor. Now that he's said it's all right to touch him, I can't help myself. I'm so cold, I lift his arm, nestling against him, as he wraps it around me, and I press my freezing hands to his abdomen.

His body is all lean muscle, his skin warm and soft like silk over hard steel. A light puff of air parts the hair on top of my head, as if he's scenting me. I lift my face to meet his. "When I touched you underwater... you spoke to me in my mind. But it wasn't as deep a connection as before, in the al'nara."

"Forgive me," he whispers. "I do not wish to scare you. I know the A'kai—"

"I'm not afraid of you, Vorek." I quickly reassure him. "What the A'kai did was... unspeakable. But, what happened between us... it was different. It didn't feel... intrusive or forced."

With his jaw set, he studies me. "Even so... I should not have linked my mind with yours. The sharing of minds is meant to be sacred—the al'nara is something only experienced between bondmates. I will make certain to maintain my mental transference shields from now on. Forgive me, Alana."

"There is nothing to forgive, Vorek."

"Tell me about the Balance," I ask, remembering how he somehow healed himself with the tree.

"My people are able to sense and connect to the lifeforce

of the earth around us. Using the Balance we're able to both give or take energy from nature."

"What about people? Are you able to transfer energy or to take from another person like you did with the tree?"

He lowers his gaze. "Many have tried to do this for their bondmates—to heal them. But they have died in the attempt. But there are rumors that this can be done between fated mates."

"Fated mates?"

"Among my people, there is something called the si'an'i-maora—the fated mate bond." His eyes meet mine intently. "Do Terrans have anything like this?"

"No. Is that how V'loryns find their mates?"

He's silent for so long, I wonder what he's thinking.

Drawing in a deep breath, I meet his gaze evenly as I ask the question I want the answer to most. "You called me Si'an T'kara. What does that mean?"

After a moment, he says, "There is something I must tell you."

"What is it?"

"You are my—"

A sinister growl echoes in the cavern from outside. We both go completely still at the sound of a voice. "He must have hidden the female. We must find her."

"We will. But, we have to tend to Damarus first. He was injured."

"I know. We will return to our territory and send scouts in the morning. The V'loryn cannot stay hidden forever. We will find them and take her from him."

Ice cold fear floods my veins, and I press myself closer to Vorek. His arms tighten around me in return. "Please," I whisper. "Don't let them take me."

"I will protect you with my life. While I draw breath, they will not touch you. My vow."

We both remain silent and still in the cave, even long after they've gone. I'm too afraid to speak or to move. "They have gone," Vorek finally whispers. "I no longer scent them nearby."

"We should leave. Try to make it to your people."

"We are still too far away. Traveling at night, we would risk encountering predators."

I swallow against the knot of worry in my stomach. "What about in the morning?"

"It is safer if we stay here a few days. They know I wish to get back to my people. They will be guarding the pass between the mountains, waiting for us to come to them."

"We have water, but what about food?"

"I will hunt," he says, matter-of-factly.

The mere thought of him leaving this cave again while the wolves are out there fills me with dread, and I tighten my arms around him. "No. I can go for a few days without eating."

He shakes his head. "You need to eat to keep up your strength. I will be fine. I—"

"You almost drowned, Vorek," I snap. "If you fall into the water again and I'm not there, you could die. You have no idea how worried I was when you left."

His eyes meet mine. "I have not thanked you for saving my life. I owe you a debt."

I take his hand in mine, threading my fingers through his. "You saved me first." I give him a faint smile. "We can call it even, all right?"

His lips quirk up slightly at the edges. "All right."

I nestle into his side.

"You should rest, Alana. I will keep watch."

"You're not tired?"

"No."

Despite my exhaustion, I tip my head up to his. "Vorek?"

"Yes?"

"Why *did* you save me?"

He arches a brow. "To which time are you referring?"

A short huff of air escapes me in a laugh. "Are you teasing me, or are you serious?"

His lips quirk up slightly at the edges and I laugh even harder.

"Do you ever fully smile?"

"No."

I shrug. "That's a shame." His brow furrows as I continue. "I think you'd probably have a very handsome smile."

He arches his brow again. "That I even have a hint of one is testimony to my time spent with Al'iro."

"Who's Al'iro?"

"One of the Aerilon that live with us." He lowers his gaze. "No, actually... he is more than that."

Now, I'm even more curious. "What do you mean?"

"He is as a brother to me—just as much family as Tavek."

"Tell me about him."

"He is a Healer—like you," he replies. "And like me... his sister was taken by the A'kai."

He hesitates a moment before speaking again. "I told you that my sister was a slave, but I did not tell you that I was one as well."

"What happened? How did you get taken?"

"In my search for my sister, I was captured and forced to fight in the gladiator rings. It is how I first met Markus and then... Al'iro." He shakes his head softly. "It is strange how we each ended up here. As if our paths were destined to have crossed... as if the goddess did this for some purpose that I do not yet understand."

"Markus is the one that claimed Lara."

"Yes. We were as close as brothers once. When we were

owned by the same master, we fought side by side in the arenas. It is how I know he is an honorable male."

"But you are no longer friends?" I ask, curious to understand.

"There is a long and terrible history of war and conflict between our two races. My people do not trust theirs. It was difficult to maintain our… friendship after we were freed, and we grew apart."

"And Al'iro?"

"Markus and I were separated when I was sold to a new master. That is when I met Al'iro. We fought together in the rings and I found out he had been captured while searching for his own sister. Together, we managed to escape."

"What of Al'iro's sister? Did he find her?"

He gives a small nod, but I note the sadness that flits briefly across his expression. "She took her own life, after we found her."

I inhale sharply. I understand this. Many times I wished for death when I was a slave. Wanting an end to all the pain.

He places two fingers up under my chin, tipping my face up to his. "Even though I was a slave, I do not claim to know all the terrible things you endured during *your* slavery. But, I ask that if you ever—" his voice catches. "If you ever fall into a despair so deep you… contemplate the taking of your own life, please know I will do all I can to help you." He cups my cheek. "Do not suffer your nightmares and your sadness in silence. Such burdens are too much for one person to carry."

Tears sting my eyes, but I blink them back. Emotions lodge in my throat, and I can't speak around them. Instead, I wrap my arms around him and hug him tightly, telling him with my embrace all the words that will not come in this moment.

Vorek is a good man. He's kind, caring, gentle, and he makes me feel safe in a way that I haven't ever since I was taken. I wake up when he moves in the night, only to return and drape one of the now-dried furs over my body and not over his. That extra bit of care makes my heart melt even more for him.

With a soft sigh, I snuggle beneath the warmth of the fur. When his arm wraps around my waist as he settles again behind me, it takes everything inside me to try to calm the frantic rhythm of my pulse as he holds me close and curls his body protectively around mine.

I can't remember the last time someone cared for me like this.

I nestle against him and close my eyes as I allow myself to drift away, surrounded by warmth and his masculine scent of cinnamon and spice.

CHAPTER 12

VOREK

*M*y people are not supposed to love.

Of all the emotions we are taught to suppress, this is the most important and considered the most dangerous. As Alana lies in my arms, I believe I understand why, for there is nothing I would not do to keep her safe. I would kill anyone who dared try to harm her and sacrifice all that I am to protect her.

My people are extremely possessive and protective of our mates. The desire to claim and possess is a primal instinct deeply embedded in our biology.

As Alana lies asleep in my arms, my possessive instincts are heightened. She is mine, and I am hers. No one will harm her while I still draw breath.

My thoughts turn again to the male she spoke of earlier—Harry, the one I suspect is probably her mate.

Even if she will never truly be mine, I will protect and defend her. I want only to be at her side and make sure she is safe. Part of me wonders if it is the bond that makes me feel this way, but another part understands it is more than just this.

My desire to claim her as my mate has only deepened in the short time we've been together, and as she instinctively nestles closer against me, I suspect it will only grow stronger.

When morning comes, the soft light of the dawning sun filters in through the curtain of water, casting sparkling reflections along the cave walls.

Alana stretches her lithe body against me, and I bite back a groan of frustration. Everything inside me demands that I claim her. She is my Si'an T'kara, and the primal need to mark and possess her fills me with longing unlike anything I've ever known.

My fangs extend into sharpened points. I desire more than anything to bind her to me in the sacred blood ritual of the *S'acris*. Need burns through me like fire, and with it comes the sudden awareness of what I fear has begun.

My mating cycle.

Closing my eyes, I draw in a deep breath and force my fangs to retract. I cannot give in to my baser instincts. No matter how much I want her, she cannot be mine. Not if she has already chosen another.

I walk toward the cave entrance and along the narrow ledge leading out from the curtain of water. My nostrils flare as I scent the wind.

"Vorek?" Alana's soft voice calls.

I move back inside. "Yes?"

"Do you sense them?"

"They are not nearby. I must use this time to hunt for food before they return."

"I'll go with you."

Fear fills me at the thought of her outside of the safety of our cave. "No. It is not safe."

"It's not safe for you, either. I don't like the idea of you going alone. What if something happens to you?"

She is right. If something happens to me, she needs to be able to reach my people.

"Come, Alana. I must show you something."

She stands and I cannot help but allow my gaze to drift over her form. She is dressed only in two small strips of cloth. One tied around her chest and the other around her pelvis and backside. As my gaze travels down her body, I stare appreciatively at the sensuous curve of her breasts and the gentle flare of her hips.

My cheeks and the tips of my ears begin to burn and I avert my gaze, worried my skin is probably now a deep shade of green.

When I finally look back, she has pulled my tunic and the furs over her small frame. I walk over to her and carefully smooth the coverings over her body and tighten the belt around her waist to secure them and keep her warm.

She smiles, and I am enchanted. "Thank you."

I dip my chin in a subtle nod and open my arms. "Come. I must carry you."

She moves closer, and I lift her into my arms. Protective instincts flood my system as she wraps her arms and legs around me.

She is mine. Mine to protect, mine to care for, mine to defend, and mine to claim.

I stop myself short, mentally chastising myself for such errant thoughts. She is not mine. She has not agreed to be. And even if I asked her, I doubt she would want me.

I push aside my desires and climb out from behind the waterfall. Using my claws, I scale the rock wall to the top and scent the wind again, scanning the snow and icy landscape around us, satisfied when I detect no sign of the Lycaons.

Carefully, I set her on her feet and gesture off into the distance. "Do you see those two mountains?"

She nods.

"The pass between them leads straight to my people."

She studies it a moment, then turns back to me.

I point up at the sky. "The sun travels in this direction, during the day. If you follow its path in the sky, you can easily find your bearings on this planet."

She listens carefully as I describe how to navigate during the day. I will show her how to use the stars as soon as night falls.

"There are many predators on this world," I continue. "One of the most common ones we encounter is the snowcat. Their fur blends with the white landscape, and they are difficult to see until they are almost upon you."

"We need another weapon," she says, surveying the area around us.

"When we return to my people, I will procure another blaster for you."

"For now, we can use this." She picks up a long, straight branch about as wide as her wrist.

I arch a brow. "If we are resorting to primitive weaponry, a rock might suffice better."

"Primitive weaponry?" she laughs. "In case you haven't noticed, we don't have much choice."

I lift my hand and extend my nails into claws. "My natural defenses are more efficient than—"

"Yes, but *I* don't have any claws or fangs"—she taps one end of the branch on the ground next to her—"so this will have to do."

I study it a moment. "It will take great force to hit something and—"

"No. I'll make a spear."

I frown as I watch her scan the riverbank, then pick up a sharp stone. She brings the edge to one end of the stick and begins scraping against it. The wood starts to peel away, and a smile tugs at my lips as I observe her.

She is clever—my Si'an T'kara.

I study her with renewed admiration.

"Where did you learn to do this?"

"My dad was in the military, too. He always taught us to be aware of our surroundings, to use whatever we could, if we were ever in a survival situation."

"He sounds like a wise man."

Sadness flits briefly across her expression. "He was."

As she blinks back tears, she turns her gaze back to me. "All right. I'm ready."

I reach for her again. "I will return you to the cave while I hunt."

"Vorek, I'm not staying behind."

"It is too dangerous for you to come. You are safer in the cave."

She steps forward and takes my hand. "It's dangerous for you, too. I want to be there to help watch out for you."

My Si'an T'kara is very brave.

"I will not risk your safety, Alana."

She places her hands on her hips. "Well, it's not your decision."

She is stubborn, too.

With stiff shoulders, I nod. "Fine."

I step toward her and present my back, crouching down slightly. "Climb on. I will carry you."

"I can walk."

I glance over my shoulder, arching a brow. "Can you run as fast as I can?"

She laughs. "No."

Considering this a loss of argument, she climbs onto my back, locking her legs around my waist and one arm around my neck, the other holding her spear.

"Hold on," I tell her before I break into a run, racing through the forest at full speed.

She holds tightly to me. A small laugh escaping her as we charge through the woods. "This is amazing," she whispers in my ear. "You're able to move so fast."

The feel of her body against mine fills me with warmth. In my mind, I can imagine a future with her… like this. The two of us together as we carve out a life on this world.

My people are no strangers to hardship. We lost our home world and settled on a barren planet. Every day since then has been a test of strength and will as we forge a new life and a new future, shaping a desert planet into something new. Even if we never manage to escape this ice world, we could still have a future here.

A familiar scent flares my nostrils and alarm bursts through me. I crest a hill, then come to an abrupt stop as it grows even stronger.

"What is it?" she asks, her voice full of concern.

"Lycaons."

Without hesitation, I extend my nails into claws and start climbing the thick trunk of a nearby tree. I dig my claws deep into the wood, not wanting to risk losing my hold and sending us tumbling to the ground.

"What are you going to do?"

"You must hold tightly to me. I am going to have to jump. It is the only way they cannot follow us. The snow is no longer falling. If we remain on the ground, our tracks will give us away."

Her grip tightens around me, and I jump to the nearest branch, advancing above ground from tree to tree. Many of these trees, I suspect, are hundreds of cycles old, their trunks so large one could build a home inside them.

I know this, because there are several scattered throughout the area where we shelter for scouting missions. I just need to locate one with an opening where we can hide.

As soon as I spot one, I send a silent prayer of thanks to the goddess. Drawing closer, I study it a moment. The opening is large enough to crawl through, and it opens up into a space big enough for the two of us to sit but not to stand. "We will hide in here until they have passed."

"Won't they be able to smell us?" she asks.

I shake my head as I point to the sap lining the inside. "This will mask our scent."

I lower myself just enough for Alana to climb off my back. As she moves around me on the larger branch, her foot slips.

She starts to fall, but I quickly wrap my hand around her arm, pulling her back up. My heart pounds in my chest. I could have lost her so easily. I usher her into the trunk opening and follow her inside, thanking the goddess for my lightning fast reflexes.

She pulls back her fur covering from her arm, and my jaw drops when I see a large red mark in the shape of my hand print. Guilt and shame flood my system. "Forgive me," I whisper, shocked and horrified that I caused her such harm.

I did not use even half my strength when I hauled her back. She is more fragile than I realized, and the thought terrifies me more than anything I've ever experienced before.

Devastation, worry, and fear all take up residence in my mind and my heart as I stare transfixed at the injury.

"It's all right, Vorek. It's just a red mark. It will go away."

I shake my head. "I hurt you, Alana."

CHAPTER 13

ALANA

Tortured emotions flit briefly across his features as he stares down at my arm. "Vorek, I'm fine. Really."

Despite my words, it's easy to see he is not convinced. "Trust me, I've had much worse than this."

I realize that's the wrong thing to say when he lowers his eyes, clenching his teeth. "I know. I just... did not want to be among those who hurt you."

I reach out and cup his cheek, drawing his attention back to me. "You've saved me more times than I can count"—I give him a warm smile—"and I've known you only a few days. So, that's saying something."

The slight upward quirk of his lips in his barely-there smile fills me with warmth. I'm glad to have eased his concern. He truly is a good man. Kind, thoughtful and caring. I never want him to believe I see him any other way because the truth is... I'm falling in love with him.

He glances at my arm again. "Your people... you are so

fragile compared to mine, Alana. I did not even use half of my strength to catch you."

I take his hand, squeezing it gently. "And that's yet another reason why I know you're such a good man."

His brow furrows as his eyes search mine.

"You are gentle where all others were not. You are kind when others have been cruel." I pause. "You make me feel safe, and that's something I have not felt ever since I was taken."

He reaches out and gently brushes a stray tendril away from my face, tucking it behind my ear, his gaze holding mine intently. "If I could, I would kill everyone who ever harmed you, Alana."

Tears sting my eyes, but I blink them back. "Thank you, Vorek."

We sit side by side and he wraps one arm around me, holding me close.

I relax against him as we wait in silence, listening for any sounds below. It occurs to me that we're in a small space and, so far, I haven't felt the familiar rush of panic that I normally feel when I'm in an enclosed space. Part of me wonders if it's because of Vorek. Because I feel so safe with him.

After a while, I whisper. "Do you think they've moved on?"

His nostrils flare as he scents the wind. "I do not smell them nearby. But, we should wait a while longer, just to be sure."

I can do that. Definitely.

I can't deny that I love being nestled against him like this. Absently, he traces his thumb in a slow circle over my upper arm as he holds me.

A cold breeze whips through our small space, and I shiver.

Without warning, he pulls me into his arms, settling my

legs across his lap as he tucks me into his chest, wrapping his fur cloak around us both in a cocoon of warmth. He doesn't speak, and neither do I.

My heart hammers in my chest. I've never been as close to a man as I've been to him over the past few days. Drawing in a deep breath, I inhale his delicious, masculine scent of cinnamon and spice. I love the feel of his strong arms around me, enveloping me completely.

Gently, he nuzzles my head. A low, rumbling sound, something like a purr, begins low in his chest. My cheeks flare with warmth, and I lift my eyes to his, blinking up at him.

"Forgive me. I… should not have—"

"It's all right," I reply quickly. "Was that a… purr?"

He arches a brow, the tips of his ears and his cheeks turning light green. "It is my *tr'llen.*"

"What is that?"

His faced flushes even darker as he averts his eyes. "It is something the males of my species do when we are… attracted to someone."

He's attracted to me?

I open my mouth to speak, but he beats me to it.

"I promise it will not happen again."

He starts to move me off his lap, but I touch his face, stopping him abruptly. "What if…" I pause, and embarrassment heats my cheeks as I struggle to push the words past my lips.

"What if… what?" he asks softly.

I trace my fingers across his brow and the tip of his left ear. A small shiver runs through him and he closes his eyes, leaning into my hand as if relishing my touch.

When he opens them again, I speak softly. "What if I'm attracted to you too?"

Surprise flits briefly across his features.

"Would that be a bad thing?" I ask.

His gaze travels over my face like a gentle caress. "No," he murmurs. "It would not."

My heart pounds as he leans in. His tr'llen purr sounds low in his chest as he skims the tip of his nose alongside mine and then across my jaw and down to the curve of my neck and shoulder.

"Your scent is intoxicating," he whispers against my skin.

I shiver slightly as heat pools deep in my core.

He pulls back. "You are cold. I must get you back to the warmth of the cave."

I smile crests my lips and I start to explain that my shiver was one of pleasure, but he carefully lifts me off his lap and moves toward the entrance.

After a moment, he turns back to me. "It is safe. We should go."

I follow him back out onto the large branch. He kneels, and I climb onto his back. As I wrap my arms and legs around him, my thoughts return to the way he touched me only a moment ago. Longing fills me at the feel of his muscular form against my body as he climbs down the tree.

He places me gently on the ground.

Something catches my eyes in the distance, and I smile as soon as I realize what it is. I break into a run toward the riverbank. "Vorek, look," I call over my shoulder. "It's our emergency pack."

He picks it up. Though it is waterlogged, he rifles through it and produces two nutrient bars, both safely wrapped in their packaging. He hands me one, and I tear it open, eating it eagerly after I dip it into the water to soften it. I smile up at him. "Now, we don't have to hunt."

He nods in agreement. "We should return to the cave," he says. "We can wait out the Lycaons, and we do not have to leave again until we go to the ship."

Relief moves through me. "I love the sound of that." And I love the idea of spending more time with him, snuggled against his body in the warmth of our cave.

He races at breakneck speed back to the cavern. I'm still in awe at how fast he can move. I close my eyes against the wave of nausea that threatens to overwhelm me as the forest around us blurs past.

When we reach the falls, he doesn't even pause before extending his claws and beginning the climb up the rock.

I'm amazed by how agile and strong he is. He moves with a sort of lethal grace I'd not expected, given his larger size compared to Terran men.

As we pass beneath the curtain of water and into the cavern mouth, I breathe a sigh of relief that we're hidden once more in the warmth and safety of our cave.

It's still light outside, so I'm able to see the back of the space clearly. The slight mist rising from the pool at the back appears inviting. I glance over my shoulder and gesture to it. "I'd like to bathe."

I remove the outer layer of furs I'm wearing, then look to him. "Can you please turn around?"

Even though we were so close earlier, I'm still not entirely comfortable at the thought of him seeing me completely unclothed yet.

He nods and walks toward the cave mouth as I carefully lift his tunic overhead and discard it on the floor beside me.

CHAPTER 14

VOREK

A small splash of water behind me tells me she's entered the pool. She releases a soft sigh of contentment, and my entire body flushes with warmth at the sound.

Closing my eyes, I swallow thickly as images of her completely undressed fill my mind. Everything inside me wants to go to her, to take her in my arms and claim her as my mate.

She said she is attracted to me. And she knows that I desire her. But I do not know if she wants to be mine completely. And before I ask, I must tell her the truth of what she is to me.

I want there to be no secrets between us. A heavy sigh escapes me as I realize this also means that I must ask her about Harry. I need to know if he is her mate. I cannot ask her to be mine if she is already taken.

I want more than anything to go to her now. To take her in my arms and seal her to me in the sacred blood ritual of the S'acris. Instead, I force myself to remain still. I must wait. I have to speak with her first.

"Vorek?" her soft voice draws my attention as I hear her stepping out of the water. "Can you please hand me one of the fur cloaks?"

I grab the closest one and walk backward, holding it behind me for her to take.

When she does, I wait patiently. "You can go next," she offers.

I go still, flaring my nostrils as I discreetly scent myself.

Does she find my smell offensive?

I did not think I smelled bad, but if she does, I must remedy this right away.

I turn to her, and my heart stutters and stops when I find her standing there wrapped in nothing but her fur cloak. My gaze drifts immediately to the elegant curve of her neck and shoulder.

My fangs extend with want to mark her—to bind her to me in the sacred blood ritual of the S'acris, but I avert my eyes. Drawing in a deep breath, I move past her and discard my pants and boots.

I wade into the water and completely submerge myself beneath it. My l'ok lengthens and extends from my body as I look toward her. Her back is facing me, her golden hair spilling down her back and shoulders. I long to run my hands through the soft, silken strands. To grip them tightly between my fingers and tip her head to one side, exposing the elegant column of her neck. To sink my teeth deep into her flesh and mark her, claiming her as my mate. To join our minds in the al'nara and my body to hers.

Drawing in a deep breath, I force myself to push away these errant thoughts and step out of the water. I wrap a fur cloak loosely around my hips, and when she turns, I do not miss the way her gaze travels appreciatively over my form.

A pink bloom spreads across her cheeks and the bridge of her nose as she stares up at me. I settle beside her and am pleased when she nestles against me for warmth.

Feeling bold, I pull her into my lap and hold her against my chest. She releases another soft sigh of contentment and rests her cheek against my collarbone. "I'm glad it's you," she whispers.

"What do you mean?"

"I'm glad that, if I had to be stranded somewhere, it's with you, Vorek."

She cups my cheek as her eyes stare deep into mine. She's so close I can feel the warmth of her breath across my skin. Her gaze drifts to my mouth. My heart hammers in my chest as she leans in and gently presses her mouth to mine.

Her lips are soft and warm. I inhale sharply as her small tongue traces along the seam of my lips, then enters my mouth. I groan as her tongue finds mine and curls around it.

"What is this?" I barely manage to breathe.

"Kissing," she whispers against my lips. "Do your people not kiss?"

"No, they do not."

She pulls back just enough for her eyes to meet mine. "Do you... like it?"

A smile tugs at my lips as I reach up and touch my fingers to the soft, plump curve of her lips, studying them intently. "Very much."

She smiles and leans in again, sealing her mouth over mine.

Myriad sensations move through me as my entire body flushes with warmth. I pull her close, wrapping my arms tightly around her.

Each movement of her tongue against mine is the most exquisite pleasure I've ever known. When she finally pulls away, I gently drop my forehead to hers.

"Alana," I whisper, cupping her face with both hands. "I lo—"

A low growl startles us both, cutting off my words. I whip my head toward the entrance to the cave and immediately pull her behind me, jumping up and facing down the A'kai stalking toward us.

A sinister grin curves his mouth. "I see you've found one of our pets."

I bare my fangs and extend my nails into deadly claws. "Leave now, or I will end you."

"Not without her," he snarls.

Rage churns deep within. "You *cannot* have her," I threaten low in my chest. "She. Is. Mine. And I will not allow you to touch her."

His brows go up in surprise. "Yours? Since when does your kind take outsiders as your mates?"

The acrid scent of Alana's fear permeates the cave, and he lifts his head, breathing deep. "I do so love the smell they emit when they are afraid. It only adds to the flavor of their delicious blood. It—"

Lightning fast, I charge him, raking my claws across his chest, drawing blood. He catches my side with his, and we tumble across the floor toward the falls.

Alana's panicked cries echo loudly, and out of the corner of my eye, I watch as she charges with her spear.

He pushes away from me and swings out his arm at Alana, but I barrel into him before he reaches her, slamming him back against the wall.

Sharp pain slices through me as his claws tear at my skin. He twists away from my grasp, and I lunge for him as he spins to face Alana. I will not allow him to hurt her.

She rushes forward, stabbing her spear into his side. He releases a deafening roar, stumbling back as he pulls it free and throws it to the ground.

He starts for her again, but I barrel into him, pushing him through the curtain of water, and we both drop over the side.

As we tumble down the falls, I catch hold of a large boulder. Lighting fast, he grabs my leg. We slam against the wall, and a terrible crack slices the air as blinding pain shoots through my calf.

I have only a moment to process my injury as the A'kai starts to pull himself up, using me as a ladder. The powerful rush of water pulls at my form, trying to rip me away, but I hold tight.

"Vorek!" Alana's panicked voice calls out above me.

The A'kai struggles to pull me down, but I kick out at him with my uninjured leg. I hit something hard and he cries out, relinquishing his grip and falling away into the water.

I glance over my shoulder and watch as he slams into a large boulder below. The crack as his head hits the stone echoes up the cliff face. Cold satisfaction fills me as his body sinks beneath the surface and obsidian blood spreads out across the water.

I am glad he is dead.

Every muscle aches, and my injured leg throbs with the effort to pull myself back up the rock wall, fighting the rushing current trying to take me.

Alana's hands wrap around my wrist as she tries to help me back up. I grit my teeth and haul myself the rest of the way. Dragging myself onto the floor, I collapse onto my back, panting heavily with exertion.

Alana drops to her knees and wraps her arms around me. She lifts her face to mine, her eyes bright with tears. "Vorek, you're hurt."

I look down at my left leg, noting the odd angle at which it now sits.

Alana pulls away the wet fur covering my lower half,

replacing it with a dry one. "Your leg is broken. I'll have to set it."

"The emergency bag," I tell her, gritting my teeth in agony. "There is a device to set bone."

She rushes to get the bag and carries it back to me. I quickly find the bone-mending device. Blinding pain shoots through me as I wrap it tight around my leg. Drawing in a deep breath, I meet her gaze evenly. "This will heal my leg, but I will be unconscious while it works."

My hand hovers over the activation button, trembling in anticipation of what is to come. I have used one of these devices before, and it was the most painful experience of my life.

Even more terrible, however, is the knowledge that I will be rendered unconscious while it works to heal me, leaving Alana vulnerable if we're attacked.

CHAPTER 15

ALANA

I t's dark outside, and there is barely enough light in the cave to make out anything on the device. Even if I could see it clearly, I don't know how to use it. "What do I need to do?"

"You must press here"—he takes my hand and guides it to a flat panel, smooth like glass—"when I tell you."

I swallow hard. "How long will you be out?"

"Several hours most likely." He pauses. "If the bone has damaged an artery, however, I—"

He stops, but I already know what he means to say. This is an emergency device. It cannot repair everything. "What about the Balance?"

He shakes his head. "There is nothing for me to take from in here. And I cannot make it down the rock wall. Not like this."

I take his hand in mine. "Can you take from me? From my lifeforce?"

His eyes widen. "It would be dangerous. I will not risk you, Alana."

"You have to, Vorek. I don't want to lose you." Panic tightens my chest. I know he said bondmates have died attempting this, but what if it works with me? What if we are fated to each other? I have dreamed of him all this time and I never told him when I should have. And now, this could be the last time I speak to him. "Please."

He cups my cheek. "Do you not know I would do anything to keep you safe? To protect you from all harm, Alana?"

A stray tear escapes my lashes and rolls gently down my cheek, and I quickly wipe it away. Leaning in, I gently brush my lips to his in a tender kiss. A faint smile curves my mouth as my fingertips gently trace the sharp line of his brow. "What did I ever do to deserve you, Vorek?"

He takes my hand and places it to his chest, directly over his heart. "I have been yours, Alana, from the first moment your eyes met mine."

My heart clenches as another tear slips down my cheek. "Is that your way of telling me you love me?"

"At first, I did not recognize it for what it was. But, I do now. You are my heart; the other half of my soul. And if the goddess comes to take me from this world to the next, I will love you, still."

I press my lips to his and whisper against them. "I love you, Vorek. Please, come back to me."

A hint of a smile curls his lips. "If the goddess comes for me, I will fight with all I am to stay with you. My vow."

I draw in a shaking breath as he gently lays back. He gives me a slight nod, and I press the button. His eyes close, and my waiting begins.

CHAPTER 16

VOREK

When I wake, I immediately sweep my gaze over the cave, searching for Alana. When I do not see her, panic sets in. I quickly remove the device from my leg and stand, glad when I do not feel even the slightest hint of pain from my injury.

I go still, listening for any sounds nearby, but only the dull, echoing roar of the falls fills the space. I flare my nostrils, drawing her delicate scent deep into my lungs. It is still strong, telling me wherever she is, she did not leave very long ago.

Carefully, I walk along the narrow ledge around the falls and immediately survey the river below. Dread stirs deep in my gut, and fear settles like a weight on my chest. She could have fallen into the water injured or been taken by the current, carried downstream, even as I stand here and do nothing. She could have ventured out of the cave and been taken by the Lycaons or another A'kai.

Myriad scenarios fill my mind, none of them good and each of them terrifying.

Terrible images assault my thoughts, setting fire to the worry within me. I struggle to calm my racing heartrate and breathing, but it is no use. She is gone, and I have no idea where she is.

I'll never forgive myself if something has happened to her. I'll—

"Vorek?"

My head whips up toward the top of the falls, in the direction of her voice. Relief floods my veins when I find her standing above me. It is short-lived, however, as she begins to climb back down.

My nails extend, and I claw my way up the rock wall to intercept her.

She lets out a surprised squeak as I gather her in my arms. "Hold onto me."

Wrapping her arms around my neck and her legs around my waist, she positions herself. "Vorek, what are you—"

"What are you doing outside of our cave?" My voice comes out harsher than I intended, but it is difficult to suppress the concern and anger as I think on all that could have happened to her out here. "You know it is not safe."

She blinks at me in disbelief before her brow furrows in anger. "I had to. We ran out of food." She gestures to the three large fish hanging from a loop on her belt.

I frown. "How did you—"

She holds up her spear, smiling proudly.

"What were you thinking?" I snap, and the expression falls from her face. "You could have died."

"I'm not completely helpless, you know." Nailing me with a piercing stare, she counters, "Are you really mad at me? I thought your people didn't express emotion, but you—"

I cut her off with a kiss, sealing my mouth over hers.

Emotions envelope me, so powerful, I can barely contain them.

She opens her mouth, and my tongue finds hers, curling around it. She runs her fingers through my hair, eagerly returning my kiss.

Unable to hold back, a connection flares brightly between us through the touch of our skin.

Fear, panic, worry, love.

I push all these emotions across the tenuous bridge, allowing her to feel the maelstrom of emotions warring within me as I think on what could have happened to her while I was unconscious.

The scent of her arousal is thick in the air, driving me mad with desire. I long to claim her as mine, and as this thought fills my mind, I allow her to feel the madness threatening to overwhelm me.

I long to possess her and be possessed. To consume her and be consumed. To join her body and her mind to mine in the sacred blood ritual of the S'acris, claiming her as my mate.

"Yes," her mind whispers to mine, having sensed my thoughts through our connection. *"I want you."*

Her words shatter the last of my control. I move quickly down the wall and back into our cave. As soon as we're inside, I press her back against the wall, pinning her with my hips. Her tongue finds mine, curling around it, deepening our kiss.

"Vorek," she breathes into my mouth.

Desire pulses through me, and I wrap my arms around her, bearing her to the floor. She is mine, and I long to claim her.

CHAPTER 17

ALANA

He moves us to the floor, pinning me beneath his much larger body, sealing his mouth over mine in a searing kiss. What he lacks in experience, he makes up for in passion, as he plunders my mouth.

He rips the fur cloak from around his hips as he moves over me. I part my thighs, and he settles between them, kissing a heated trail down my neck. I thread my fingers through his hair, and a low moan escapes me when he cups his hand over my breast.

When he lifts his head, I inhale sharply as he stares down at me. His eyes are obsidian black, and his canines are extended into sharpened points.

The moment he notices my fear, his eyes turn glowing green once more, and he moves off of me and to the side, pulling one of the fur cloaks around him to cover his manhood. "Forgive me, Alana. I did not mean to scare you, I—"

I press a finger to his lips to silence him. "It's all right," I whisper.

His brow furrows. "I could scent your fear."

I lean in and press a tender kiss to his lips, then rest my forehead to his. "I just wasn't prepared. But, now I know what you look like when..." I allow my voice to trail off as heat flushes my cheeks. "I'm not afraid. I trust you. Completely."

His expression softens a moment before the hunger returns to his eyes. I cup the back of his neck, bringing his mouth back down to mine. Our lips meet in a passionate kiss, repeatedly meshing and stealing the breath from my lungs.

He takes my hand, and desire flares brightly between us as need and longing flow across the connection.

He groans as my tongue strokes against his, and I can feel the desire and hunger burning through him, just as I know he feels mine when he rolls his hips against my center, his length is hard against my inner thigh and so close to where I want him to be.

He rips his mouth from mine and stares down at me, his gaze full of fire and possession. "You are certain you want me?"

"I—"

Through the touch of our hands, I feel him searching our connection for the answer even as my lips refuse to move, unsure how to say what I mean. I love him, but I've never done this before, and I'm afraid. Not because I fear him, but because this is new. I glance down at his length, hard, erect and lined with ridges, reminding me he is alien.

"My *l'ok*," he says, and I realize he is speaking of his manhood. "Is it very different from Terran males?"

I've never made love before, but from the images I've seen it doesn't look all that strange from a Terran. "The shape is the same but much larger, I think, and the ridges are... different."

"We do not have to do anything you do not wish, Alana," he says softly. "I will never ask for more than you are willing to give."

"Can we just... touch for now?" I ask, my cheeks heating in embarrassment when I'm held captive by his eyes.

He reaches down and tenderly brushes the hair back from my face.

Golden like the sun and soft as silkara—his thoughts fill my mind in the al'nara as he runs his fingers gently through my hair and studies my face. *"You are perfect."*

Smoothing his hand down my body, he traces his fingers lightly over my skin, leaving a trail of fire in their wake. He stares down at me as if I'm a rare and precious treasure. "There are no words in my language," he whispers, "to convey the beauty of your face, your luminous eyes, and your smile that radiates as brightly as the sun."

"Alana," his mind whispers to mine again, full of awe-filled reverence as he stares down at me. *"You are perfect."*

I run my fingers over the hard planes of muscle lining his abdomen and chest. My gaze drops to his *l'ok*. I wrap my fingers around him, and gasp when I realize they don't quite reach.

He groans as I run my thumb over the tip, catching the small bead of liquid gathering on the end. He takes my hand, locking eyes with me, and moves my thumb down my lower abdomen, marking me with his scent.

Through our connection, something dark and primal rises within him at this gesture, clawing its way to the surface and threatening to break free. This part of him desperate to claim and possess me: mind, body and soul. *"Tell me you are mine."*

"Yours," I breathe.

He captures my mouth in a searing kiss, stealing the breath from my lungs. *"Show me how to touch you, Alana. I want only to give you pleasure."*

CHAPTER 18

VOREK

She takes my hand and guides it to her breast. As I cup the soft mound beneath my palm, she arches up into my touch. I close my mouth over the peak, tasting the sweet salt of her skin.

She moans as I lave my tongue across the hard bead and threads her fingers through my hair. Her fingers trace over the pointed tips of my ears, sending small shivers of pleasure down my spine.

I groan as the scent of her arousal grows thick in the air, and move down her body and the soft dip of her abdomen to her mons. I smooth my hands up her inner thighs, carefully opening her to me.

"May I kiss you here?"

She stares at me through a heavy-lidded gaze and nods.

I dip my head between her thighs and drag my tongue between her already slick folds, tasting the sweet nectar of her warm, wet heat.

When I reach the top, a low moan escapes her as my

tongue moves over a pearl of softly hooded flesh. I tease around it, listening to the small sounds of pleasure she makes, and concentrate my effort on the places that make her entire body light up with pleasure.

She digs her heels into my back, arching up against me. She pulls on my shoulders, and I move back up her body, sealing my mouth over hers in a claiming kiss.

She takes my hand and guides it to her slick folds. When I reach the small bundle of nerves at the top, a low moan escapes her.

Through our connection I can feel each response of her body to my touch, learning what she likes best. She guides me to her entrance. Carefully, I insert one finger. A soft moan leaves her mouth, and I add another when I sense her desire for more.

In her mind, I understand all of this is just as new to her as it is to me. I now know she is not claimed by another, and I want to roar my happiness to the stars that she is not already taken.

I stroke my fingers back and forth inside her. She moans as pleasure coils tight in her core. "Please, Vorek," she whispers, and I understand through the connection she is close to her peak.

I seal my mouth over hers, and brush my thumb over the bundle of nerves that make her cry out in pleasure. The small muscles of her channel begin to flex and quiver around my fingers. The scent of her arousal is overwhelming, and a low growl rumbles my chest as she moves closer to the edge.

Her entire body goes taut a moment before the muscles of her core clamp down around my fingers as she cries out my name and finds her release.

With our minds joined, I experience the height of her climax as wave after wave of pleasure washes over and through her entire body.

When I gently pull away, she stares up at me, breathless and panting. "That was… there are no words," she breathes.

I pull her against me, holding her close. My l'ok is a hard bar between us. She lifts her head to me. "You didn't—"

I brush my lips to hers. "I want the first time I release to be when I am inside you."

She kisses me again and nestles into my embrace.

Gently, I smooth my hand down her back, stopping as my fingers trace over the deep, jagged scars that mar her delicate flesh.

She stills, and through our link, I can sense her concern. She believes I will find her ugly because of this. So, I move to reassure her.

I cup her chin and lift her eyes to mine. "You are the most beautiful female I have ever seen. If I could, I would kill everyone who ever harmed you or touched you against your will."

I take her hand, entwining our fingers. "There is something I must tell you."

"What is it?"

CHAPTER 19

ALANA

With tension apparent in his face, his eyes meet mine. "You are my Si'an T'kara. My fated one. I do not know how it is possible, but I feel it here." He pulls our joined hands to his bare chest, resting my open palm over his beating heart. "I was drawn to find you, and, now... I understand why. The moment your eyes first met mine, I felt the pull of the sacred bond between us—the si'an'inamora. It has not happened in over two-thousand cycles. It was believed to be myth, but now I understand it is real."

"Is that why you saved me?"

He shakes his head. "It is more than that. When I first saw you stand against the A'kai who was your captor, I've never admired someone as much as I did you, in that moment. You have a rare strength. You are intelligent and... despite your smaller size, you are strong in ways I could scarcely imagine, before I met you." He pauses. "I desire to take you as my bondmate, Alana. And I would want you, even without the fated bond."

I cup his cheek. "I dreamed of you."

His brow furrows softly.

I continue. "When I first saw you, I knew." I trace my fingers across his brow and then cup his cheek. "I have drawn your face so many times, I recognized you immediately. In my dreams, you called me your Si'an T'kara, but I did not know what it meant."

"How is this possible?" he whispers. "Do your people possess the gift of precognition?"

"I don't know," I answer honestly. "I only know that my mother dreamed of my father before they met. And when she finally saw him, they fell in love at first sight. I never believed it was possible to fall for someone so quickly, but... that's what has happened with you." I search his glowing, green eyes. "I've fallen in love with you, Vorek." I pause. "My dreams of you... they are what kept me alive when it would have been easier to give up. You were my light in the darkness."

He leans in, pressing his lips to mine in a tender kiss. "You are mine, Alana, and I am yours. I long to seal you to me in the sacred blood ritual of the S'acris and take you as my bondmate."

I want to be his, but I have so many questions. "What is the S'acris?"

"It is the claiming," he replies. "The sealing of our blood and our souls. On the night of our bonding ceremony, we mark our mates." He touches the curve of my neck and shoulder and then traces his finger over the pulsing artery of my neck. "We drink of their blood to seal ourselves to each other as we join our minds in the al'nara and our bodies as one. It creates a permanent mental bond between us."

I search his eyes. "So, that would mean, you'd always be able to read my mind? Sense my thoughts?"

"In a way," he explains. "I have heard it is similar to the familial bond but much stronger. A gentle hum in the back of one's mind that is the presence of the other."

I frown as I consider this. "But, I'd still be me, right? Or would I… become someone else? Someone that is both you and me and—"

He shakes his head. "We do not lose who we are through the connection. It only makes the bond between us that much stronger. Unbreakable. It tethers our minds, souls, and bodies. If one dies, the other usually follows shortly after."

"Is this how it works with other species that bond with your people?"

"My kind do not take mates outside of our race. We would be the first."

My lips part in wonder.

He pulls me to his chest. "We do not have to rush anything. Until you are certain, we will remain as we are. And even if—" his voice catches. "Even if you decide not to bond with me, I will still protect you and watch over you, Alana."

I wrap my arms around him and brush my lips against his. "I love you, Vorek. I just… I'm afraid."

Sadness flashes briefly behind his eyes. "Of me?"

"No," I quickly reassure him. "I have terrible memories of the A'kai." I move my hair to one side, revealing the place on my neck where Novan sank his fangs deep into my flesh. "I know you are not like them. But, I'm worried that when you seal us, I'll go back to that place in my mind. And… I don't want to go back there. Not now."

Gently, he drops his forehead to mine. "Then, we will wait for however long you need to decide. I will never ask you to do something you do not wish. Nor will I ever touch you without your consent."

I trace my fingers across the thick bands of muscle that line his chest. "Then, can we just touch each other and kiss for now?"

A smile tugs at his lips. "Yes."

We spend the rest of the night kissing and exploring each other. He takes my hand, and we sink deep into the al'nara. We swim through an ocean of our combined thoughts, and I realize that what he feels for me is so much more than love.

The si'an'inamora is deep as an ocean and constant as the stars. It is an irrevocable truth known deep in the soul. It will not falter or fade, and it will admit no other.

As I fall asleep in his arms, I realize that I have never felt more loved than I do in this moment with him.

Just as I drift away, a piercing howl fills the air, startling us both. Vorek scrambles to his feet, and I do the same.

His eyes are wide. "We must leave. They are too close; we do not have a choice."

I pull several furs over me, along with the shoes he made, as he dresses quickly in his pants and boots, throwing a fur cloak around his shoulders to cover his bare torso, "What are we going to do?"

"We have no choice but to try to outrun them. To make it to the mountain pass and hope my communicator is close enough to transmit our location to my people and the Aerilon."

"What if it doesn't work?"

He places both hands on my shoulders. "Then, I will distract them while you hide. Continue on in the direction I've shown you, and you will make it."

I shake my head. "No, I won't leave you."

"We do not have time to argue. We must go. *Now*."

I strap the emergency pack across my shoulders, then climb onto his back.

He scales the falls, and as soon as we reach the top, he breaks into a run, heading straight for the mountains in the distance.

A chorus of howls echoes behind us, and as I glance over my shoulder, my heart stops at the sight of the pack of wolves in pursuit, following close on our heels.

CHAPTER 20

ALANA

I hold tightly to Vorek as we race through the forest. The trees are a blur as we rush past, and I'm surprised, once again, at how the wolves are able to keep pace with his V'loryn speed.

Vorek says they are not as strong as him, but there are at least five behind us. My pulse pounds in my ears. Whatever happens, I won't leave him. Even if he tells me to run.

I would rather die fighting than leave him to face them alone.

The mountains rise up before us, the narrow trail cutting between them filling me with fear. If the Lycaons are anything like the wolves of Terra, they hunt in packs.

It is not unusual for them to herd prey into a trap, and as we race through the mountain pass, dread twists deep in my gut. "Vorek, there are only three behind us. What if this is a trap?"

He skids to a halt and extends his claws. Without warning, he begins to climb the mountain face on the left. The angle is steep, and if we fall from here, I know I wouldn't survive.

An angry howl behind us is followed by a deep rumbling growl. "Give us the female!"

"No!" Vorek yells over his shoulder. "She is mine! You *will not* touch her!"

"We won't allow you to harm her, V'loryn."

"Harm her?" he counters. "She is my mate!"

I glance behind me to find a stunned look upon the wolf's face. His glowing orange eyes wide as they stare up at me.

My heart hammers as Vorek climbs even higher. A scraping of rock behind us draws my attention, and I glance over my shoulder to see two more of the wolves scaling the rock wall, determined to reach us.

A low growl rumbles Vorek's chest as we continue to ascend. When we reach a small plateau, he taps his wristband. A green light appears on the display. "Help is coming, Alana. We'll be all right."

The Lycaons are gaining and nearly upon us. Despite my fear of falling, I reach for a nearby loose rock and throw it down at them, trying to keep them at bay.

The closest one, with glowing orange eyes, claws his way up onto the plateau. My heart stops. The wolf is more than three times the size of Vorek. Its gaze darts to mine, and Vorek wraps his hand around my forearm, pulling me behind him.

The wolf snarls, baring two rows of gleaming, sharp, white fangs. "Give me the Terran."

Vorek's nails lengthen into claws and his canines extend into sharpened points. I watch as his eyes turn obsidian black.

Vampire. The word surfaces in my mind, stealing the breath from my lungs.

"She. Is. Mine." A deep growl rumbles in Vorek's chest. "You *will not* touch her."

The wolf lunges and Vorek meets him head on, their bodies crashing like thunder as their movements become a deadly blur of fangs and claws.

Vorek pins the Lycaon to the ground and I watch as the wolf writhes beneath him, struggling to break free of Vorek's iron embrace.

Panic squeezes my chest as I glance over the edge of the plateau and see three more wolves nearly here. "Vorek, more are coming!"

A fluttering noise overhead grabs my attention, and I lift my gaze to see two men—aliens—one with pale-green skin and the other violet, with wings similar to a dragonfly, hovering above us.

"Al'iro!" Vorek calls out. "Take Alana!"

The violet male swoops down, wrapping his hands around my waist, and my heart slams in my throat. I'm afraid to let go, but I force myself to relinquish my hold on Vorek, worried I might cause him to fall.

I'm pulled away into the sky and watch as the green-skinned male swoops down and gathers up Vorek.

The newly freed Lycaon leaps into the air, snapping his massive jaws and barely missing catching Vorek's leg.

The Lycaons growl their displeasure as they watch us ascend up into the clouds and far away from them.

Above the cloud line, I cannot see how far we are from the ground, and I'm relieved. My stomach is already twisted in a violent knot as I imagine tumbling to my death. "Please don't drop me." The words escape my mouth before I even realize I've said them aloud.

"You are safe. I promise I would never allow you to fall," his voice resounds above me.

"Thank you..."

"You are Terran, are you not?"

"Yes."

"Your people are very similar to the V'loryns."

"We were mistaken as them many times, while we were slaves."

He's quiet a moment before he replies. "You are safe here with us. We will not allow you to be taken ever again."

Emotions lodge in my throat. "Thank you."

Up ahead, a large ship comes into view. Covered in a layer of snow and ice, it appears mostly intact, and I wonder how it was able to land in one piece. It is nothing short of impressive. It appears sleek, powerful, and beautifully designed. The platinum-colored metal of the exterior hull is polished to sparkling clarity and I cannot understand how it managed to crash intact like this.

Several people are standing around outside, and as we approach, I notice a strange shimmering reflection around it —almost like a soap bubble.

It disappears as we draw closer, and I watch as it reappears behind us. "A shield?"

"Yes, for defense. To keep out our enemies. It is what kept the ship intact as well, cushioning it as it crashed."

As soon as we land, he turns toward me, dipping his chin in greeting. "I am Al'iro. What is your name?"

Vorek walks up beside me. Wrapping a possessive arm around my waist, he tugs me close to his side. I don't miss the way Al'iro's eyes widen slightly. "I'm Alana."

Al'iro opens his mouth to speak, but a low growl rumbles Vorek's chest and Al'iro steps back two paces, his gaze watching my normally stoic V'loryn boyfriend warily.

I turn to Vorek and his green eyes swirl with black as his canines extend into sharp fangs as he glares at the man he claims is his friend. "Vorek, what's wrong?"

He blinks several times as if coming back to himself. His

eyes return to their normal glowing green and something akin to guilt and shame flit across his face. "Forgive me," he murmurs.

Al'iro approaches cautiously. "Vorek, is this the beginning of—"

"No," Vorek says quickly. "My protective instincts are simply... still elevated from my fight with the Lyacaon."

Al'iro frowns. "Maybe I should scan you. Make sure that you're all right."

He shakes his head. "I am already healing."

I glance down at his arms and notice the skin is already knit back together from where he was bitten and clawed by the Lycaon.

"Alana is the one who should be scanned. She has been through much and I want to make certain she is well."

"I'm fine, Vorek," I insist. "Nothing is wrong."

His gaze travels over my form and the several scratch marks across my arms and legs. "Please, Alana. Al'iro is a Healer. Allow him to treat you."

My heart melts at his concern. "All right."

Another man comes up to us, and I smile as soon as I recognize him. "You must be Tavek."

He cocks his head to the side to regard me, his gaze traveling over Vorek's arm around my waist. "I am. How did you know?"

"Vorek told me." I smile. "And you look like twins, almost. I'm Alana."

He dips his chin in a subtle bow. "It is agreeable to meet you, Alana."

His gaze sweeps to Vorek. "We were worried for you. I am glad you have returned." He returns his attention to me. "I assume my brother has told you all good things about me." He arches a teasing brow. "Am I correct?"

"Yes," I laugh softly. "All good things."

Another growl vibrates Vorek's chest and his brother's eyes flash with alarm. "Brother, what is wrong?"

Drawing in a deep breath, Vorek shakes his head. "Nothing, I am fine."

He keeps saying this, but I don't think so. Something is wrong and I don't think it's some lingering effect of having fought the Lycaon.

Vorek turns to him. "I am simply... on edge. Al'iro needs to scan Alana and tend her injuries."

Tavek's gaze holds Vorek's a moment more, a question behind his eyes. "Of course," he finally says. "That is... understandable."

Vorek turns to Al'iro. "Shall we?"

As we follow Al'iro, Tavek trails behind us. Several pairs of glowing, green eyes watch us with intense fascination—all the V'loryns staring at me like I'm the most interesting thing they've ever seen.

Vorek's arm tightens around my waist and another growl rumbles his chest, but quickly stops when my head snaps up to his.

The Aerilon watch me as well, but their eyes are various shades of reflective gold and silver. In contrast to the stoic masks of the V'loryns, they smile warmly at me as I pass. Their dragonfly like wings tucked close to their backs.

When we enter the ship, I stare gaping at all the smooth, polished silver metal and glass. It's all rounded corners and soft edges. Even though Vorek explained how they were able to land intact, I'm still surprised everything seems to work. A soft white glow emits throughout, lending an organic warmth to the space.

We reach what I assume is the med bay, and my jaw drops as I take everything in. I remember thinking the med bay of my ship was impressive, but this easily eclipses anything I've ever seen before.

Sparkling panels, crystal clear glass, and the soft hint of aseptic cleaner in the air all remind me of where I used to work, but that is where the similarities end. Several beds line the space, and I note the large displays over each one.

Al'iro instructs me to lie down. As soon as I do, a casing begins to close over me. Panic stops my heart. I'm not good in enclosed spaces, especially ones as small as this. Not after all my time spent in cages and cells.

Dark memories flood my thoughts as fear twists deep inside me. Unable to stop myself, I pound on the glass, and cry out, "Vorek!"

He growls at Al'iro, ordering him to open it again.

Al'iro's face is flustered, and he quickly taps a series of commands into the panel. It feels like an eternity as it slowly opens. My pulse pounds in my ears, and my breathing is short and clipped by the time it fully retracts.

I jerk up, wrapping my arms around Vorek so tight, if he were a Terran man, he'd probably complain I'm choking him.

Instead, he lifts me into his arms and cradles me to his chest. "You are safe, Alana. It is a Med Repair Unit. We use the MRUs to assess injuries and run scans."

I'm ashamed of my fear, but even so, I can't help it. I've been through too much. Tears escape my lashes as I try to will myself to calm.

He sits down on another bed, settling me into his lap and tenderly touching my cheek, brushing away my tears. He takes my hand, and a wave of comfort and warmth flows across the tenuous bond along with his whispered words in my mind. *You are safe. I will allow no harm to come to you. My vow.*

I cup his face, and he drops his forehead to mine.

Al'iro approaches us and bows low, his golden eyes filled with regret. "Forgive me. I did not think. I should have realized that this might upset you."

"It's all right, I just need a moment."

"We do not have to use the MRU, Alana. I can take care of whatever injuries you have with—"

"But, if you scan me, you'll have Terran anatomy in your database then, right?"

"Yes."

"I am a doctor—Healer—I correct. I understand how important it is to know something about anatomy before you treat a patient."

A smile curls his lips. "A fellow Healer. It will be good to have more Healers here."

I love that he doesn't appear to look down on me for my fear.

I turn to Vorek. "All right. I can do this. Now that I know what to expect, I'm prepared."

His eyes flash with concern. "You do not have to do this."

"I want to, Vorek. When we start finding more of my people, we'll need to be able to treat them. If the MRU scans me, it can start building a database on my anatomy and physiology."

His eyes sweep to Al'iro, narrowing. "If there are any problems, open the casing immediately."

Al'iro blinks several times as he stumbles over his words. "Of—of course, Commander."

I move back to the bed and lie down. As the MRU closes over me, I draw in a deep breath and slowly exhale through my nostrils, fighting against the panic threatening to overwhelm me. Vorek places his palm on the clear casing, and I put my hand up to the glass. His eyes are full of concern and so much love and devotion, my heart melts.

CHAPTER 21

VOREK

As the scanner travels over Alana's form, I place my hand to the glass, and she does the same, reaching out for the comfort of one another, even if through a barrier. Watching the display, anger floods my veins as Al'iro points out all her healed injuries from her time as a slave.

If I could, I would kill everyone who ever hurt her and touched her against her will.

Several healed fractures are visible all throughout her body, and the deep, jagged slave markings scar her back. These were made with silic-acid—deliberately permanent—and cannot be removed. Not even with an MRU. Usually, the Zovians and Anguis make these, but in her marred flesh, I recognize the A'kai glyphs.

Blood breeder.

Al'iro's eyes are wide as they meet mine. "The A'kai not only wanted her people for their blood, they also wanted to breed them."

"We must find the others," I tell him. "As soon as possible."

My free hand curls into a fist at my side as I think on all she has endured. My Si'an T'kara is brave and stronger than I realized. I am ashamed of all the times I ever thought her fragile, for it is clear to me, now, she is anything but.

Al'iro turns to me, his golden eyes full of concern. "I have heard your people are extremely possessive of their mates. In my study of your medical literature, I have also found that this instinct is heightened around the time of the mating cycle."

As his gaze holds mine, I recognize that his statement is also a question. With a slight clench of my jaw, I lower my gaze. "I believe I may be in the early stages of my mating cycle. My emotions have become... volatile, of late." I place my hand on the MRU casing, staring down at the unconscious form of my mate. "She is mine, Al'iro. My Si'an T'kara."

He blinks several times. "You are certain?"

"Yes. And I believe this is why my cycle has come." I run a hand roughly through my hair. "It is even more difficult to maintain my emotional controls with so many unbonded males around us now."

He reaches out as if to place a hand on my shoulder, but stops. "Then, I suggest you either seclude yourself or claim her. You cannot continue in this way. From what I have read, your aggression and your primal instincts will only continue to grow stronger until you lose control entirely."

I curl my hands into fists at my side to still their shaking. Need burns through me like fire, and I struggle to push it back down. I shift my attention to her scans and gesture to them. "I suspect you will find that her species is fragile compared to ours. She has agreed to become my mate, but our... differences concern me. I will not risk hurting her. I will wait to claim her after my cycle has passed."

"And when it comes again?" Al'iro asks. "I have read that your kind experience this every three cycles."

"Once the permanent mental bond of the S'acris is in place, I will be as aware of her body as I am of my own. This is how V'loryn males are able to retain some semblance of control during the mating cycle with their mates. But I cannot risk forming the S'acris with her now. Not as I am. Not while my ability to maintain my control is compromised like this."

"What will you do?"

"I will seclude myself. But before I do, I must speak with her. Explain what is happening. I do not want to simply disappear for several days without telling her."

He nods. "Fine. But do not delay. This will only grow more difficult as time goes on."

When the scan is finished, Al'iro studies the read out, his brow creased in concern. He opens the casing and I pull Alana back into my arms, running my hand soothingly across her back and shoulders.

"What is it?" I ask him.

"There is a tracker at the base of her neck, along her spine."

My mouth drifts open. I wonder if that is how the A'kai found us in the cave.

"Can you remove it?" she asks.

"Yes, but I will have to sedate you."

"Do it," she states firmly. "I want it out. I don't want them to have any way to track me."

He dips his chin. "Of course."

Gently, she squeezes my hand. With her palm against mine, I carefully open a connection between us. Despite her resolve, fear lingers in the back of her mind. As a Healer, she understands the risks associated with any procedure.

She turns to me. "Will you—" she stops short and I can

sense what she holds back. She wants me to stay with her, but she believes it would be selfish to ask this of me for some reason.

But she is my mate. Why would I leave her side? Especially when she wishes me to remain with her through something like this.

"Always, my Si'an T'kara," I whisper, pulling her close. Gently, I drop my forehead to hers. "I will not leave your side."

She smiles and brushes her lips to mine in a tender kiss.

As Al'iro cuts into her flesh, it is difficult to watch.

His golden eyes flick up to mine. "She will be fine, Vorek."

"She has been through so much," I whisper. Anger fills me as my gaze travels over the markings across her back.

He frowns as he studies the read out. "Her people do not possess even half the strength of either of our races," he says. "They are so fragile compared to us."

I clench my jaw as anger burns through me when I think on her abuse at the hands of the A'kai. "We have allowed the A'kai to live so long as they kept to their territory, but we can no longer afford to do this now. Not with Alana's people here. The A'kai are a threat to their safety."

Al'iro frowns. "What do you intend to do?"

"We will find them, and we will end them."

"As a Healer I know that it is wrong to take life but, in this case... I cannot find it in me to argue on their behalf. The A'kai are cruel and ruthless beings." His gaze drifts to the screen and the read out of all the injuries Alana suffered at their hands. "We have to protect the Terrans."

"Brother," Tavek's voice comes from behind me.

I turn to face him, my hand still holding Alana's while she sleeps.

"I could not help but overhear." His brow furrows deeply. "You called her your Si'an T'kara."

"It is truth. I felt the pull of the fated bond the moment her eyes met mine."

Tavek's gaze sweeps to her. "But... she is not V'loryn."

"It matters not," I tell him. "She is mine and I am hers."

He darts a look at her neck, no doubt searching for my mark. "Have you sealed her to you in the S'acris?"

"Not yet."

He places a hand on my shoulder. "I am happy for you, Brother."

A smile tugs at my lips. "Thank you." I pause. "Where are we with the search for the rest of her people?"

"We have found none so far. But, we are still searching."

"Instruct the others to extend the search perimeter. I found her far outside of our territory."

He dips his chin in a firm nod, and leaves to relay my orders.

I sit in a chair next to Alana's bed while she sleeps. After what feels like forever, she begins to stir gently. I watch with great anticipation and relief as her eyelids flutter and open.

"Vorek," she says my name weakly, a faint smile curving her lips. "How did I do?"

I lean down and press a tender kiss to her forehead. "You did well, my Si'an T'kara."

Al'iro runs the scanner over her again, checking the read out thoroughly. "Everything appears all right, but you should rest. And tomorrow, if you would like, we can begin your training with our equipment. It would be a blessing to have another Healer among our people."

She smiles. "I'd like that too."

She turns to me and it is easy to read the exhaustion in her features. I take her hand in mine. "Can you walk?"

"Yes."

As we walk to my quarters, I inform her about the search for her people. "I instructed that we expand the search perimeter. It seems the A'kai and the Lycaons are both hunting Terrans."

She stops and turns to me. "Before the Aerilon helped us, one of the Lycaons... I don't think they want to hurt me, Vorek. His words... he thought they were trying to save me. From you."

I clench my jaw. I have considered this as well. Even so, I would not have given her to them. "I do not want them near you until we know more about their intentions."

"I agree," she says. "But maybe you could reach out to them. Find out if they have seen any others like me."

"I will send someone to speak with them."

She squeezes my hand. "And maybe when we go to see Lara, we can convince the Mosaurans to help us."

"If they agree, they would be good allies. But, I do not know if they will."

"Why not?"

"There are many unresolved issues between us."

"Like what?"

I open my mouth to respond, but Kyvan—one of our ship's engineers—walks up to me. I don't miss the way his gaze darts discreetly to Alana before he speaks. I'm sure they are all curious about her. No doubt, my brother has already begun spreading the information that she is my Si'an T'kara.

"The unit is requesting permission to begin night searches for the Terrans."

I clench my jaw. "It is dangerous. In addition to the A'kai and Lycaons, there are many nocturnal predators on this world."

"We will go in pairs, Commander."

His eyes sweep to Alana once more, and I know my suspicions are correct. Word has already spread of Alana being my fated one. This gives hope to the rest of the males under my command. It is the secret desire of almost every V'loryn to be blessed with the fated bond of the si'an'inamora.

"Fine. But, no more than four at a time, and you must stay within range of the communicators when out at night. You may begin these patrols tomorrow evening. Tonight, we will hold a briefing, once the others return from their search."

He bows. "Of course, Commander."

CHAPTER 22

ALANA

On the way to Vorek's quarters, we get stopped a few more times by his men. As Commander, it's easy to see Vorek has a great responsibility here, and they've missed him while he was gone.

Already, I miss the time we had when it was just the two of us. I wonder, now, if we'll ever get any time alone. I can't deny, however, how proud I am as I watch him interact with his men. He exudes confidence and authority, but he also listens very carefully to what each person has to say.

As someone who was in the military, I recognize the qualities of a good and adept leader when I see one.

He leads me down the end of a long hallway and stops in front of what appears to be a blank wall. He lifts his palm and presses it to the metal, and a lighted outline of a door appears and slides open. He takes my hand and places my palm to the same spot—a very slight indentation in the metal panel. "Now, it is coded to you, Alana. You should have no trouble coming and going."

"If I can find it," I tease.

He frowns. "Can you not see the door?"

I look again at the wall. "Not until the light outlined it."

He blinks several times. "Your visual spectrum must not be as wide as ours." He turns to the door. "We will have to mark them in some way for your people to see them."

I love how he is already planning for a future that includes finding more Terrans and bringing them here. He's determined to find them all and rescue any still being held by the A'kai.

I just pray they're all found soon.

I'm desperate to see Lara, to hear about what she went through and ask her about the Mosaurans. I'd always heard of them, but never saw them, when I was a slave. They are anti-slavery, like the V'loryns and the Aerilon, so, they can't be bad people.

I'm about to ask Vorek more about them, but when we step inside, I'm surprised by how large this space is. It's palatial, to say the least. A large bed on the opposite wall of the floor-to-ceiling viewscreen draws my attention. It's unlike anything I've ever seen.

A massive, white, rounded canopy curves overhead, reminding me of a large, but open, cocoon. The bedding is covered with a shimmering, silver material, embroidered in white thread, with an intricate pattern of curling vines with heart-shaped leaves.

It looks so inviting and romantic that heat blooms across my cheeks at the mere thought of sharing the bed with Vorek.

A desk in the far corner and a table with two chairs appear to be made from ornately carved wood, lending an almost fairy-tale-like appearance to the space. Everything about this ship is a strange mixture of technology and intricately sculpted elegance.

Another door leads into the cleansing room, complete with a shower, sink, and toilet that come out from the wall with the touch of a button.

When he shows me the ion shower, I'm both impressed and amazed. By activating a simple control panel, I feel a slight tingling across my skin, and when I look down, every speck of dirt is gone from my body, as well as his, and we didn't even have to undress.

"There is an option to use water as well," he explains. "But this is normally much faster."

I like the idea of a warm shower, and I'll have to definitely try it later.

When we walk back into the bedroom, Vorek slips his arms around me, pulling me back against the solid wall of his chest. Gently, he nuzzles my temple and presses a kiss to my cheek.

I gesture to the lights and the cleansing room. "It's amazing that all of this still works."

"Our engines were damaged by our descent into the wormhole. We diverted the ship's power to all other systems. Everything still functions on the ship but the engines. We are still working on figuring out a way to repair them. We have not given up yet." He pauses. "We scout for other ships and wreckage, salvaging parts to try to retrofit them to our vessel. I have confidence we will someday find what we need."

"What about the others? Have you talked with the other races to see if you might be able to work together to repair one of your ships and leave this place?"

"I have considered it, but I doubt we could all agree on this. The Lycaons are too savage, and so are the A'kai. The Mosaurans are volatile and aggressive—they refuse to see reason on many occasions. The Aerilon... they are the only ones capable of rational thought."

JESSICA GRAYSON & ARIA WINTER

He turns to a console, on the wall near the bed, and presses a button to activate it. With a flick of his wrist, he projects an image of a man with scales and wings. "What is that?"

"That is a Mosauran."

"Mosauran," I whisper, more to myself than to him as I think of Lara. I can hardly believe she's married to one of them. I watch as the picture changes into what looks like a fire-breathing dragon. My jaw drops. "They look like dragons when they shift forms."

"Strange," he says. "Your word for them is similar to what they call themselves in this form. Draken," he explains.

I turn to him. "But I saw one in your mind... when we were in the al'nara and you showed me your world."

"Those are different," he explains. "They are *v'rachs,* and they do not shift. They are also much larger than the Mosaurans when they shift into their four-legged form."

I study the image closely. "Your people and the A'kai are similar to Vampires—creatures we thought were only myths."

His brow furrows deeply. "Perhaps our kind visited your world in the past. Along with the Mosaurans."

He projects another image of the werewolf creatures and I stare in astonishment as it transforms into something that appear similar to a Terran male, but with pointed ears and glowing orange eyes. "I didn't realize they looked like this," I tell him.

"They are shifters, like the Mosaurans. Able to easily change forms."

I shake my head in disbelief. "They look like werewolves and the Aerilon like the Fae. Creatures that my people believed were made up by ancient storytellers." I pause. "Vorek, I think you're right. Your people and theirs, they

must have come to Terra at some point. And if they did…
maybe one of them knows where it is."

He takes my hand. "We will not stop trying to find a way
off this world. And when we do, I will help you find your
planet. But for now, we will search for your people who have
crashed here."

I wrap my arms around him, hugging him close. "But
what happens if we leave here? Would your people accept
me? Accept us? You said that none of them has ever taken a
mate outside of your race."

"We have the fated bond between us, Alana." He gently
smooths a hand over my hair and down my back as he holds
me to his chest. "It is a sacred blessing from the goddess that
has not been found in over two thousand cycles. You are my
mate. No one will ever part us. My vow."

He pulls back just enough to meet my gaze. "What of your
people? Would they accept me?"

"I don't know," I admit. "My people have never traveled
outside of our planetary system. We've never encountered
any other space-faring species before."

Despite his impassive expression, the shock is easily read
in his eyes.

I shake my head softly. "I feel like there's so much I don't
know. All these species and worlds that exist that I never
even knew about before."

"I will teach you about my people, Alana. So that when we
leave this planet and return to V'lora, you will already know
what awaits us."

A smile crests my lips. "I'd like that, Vorek."

He flips to another image on the screen. A V'loryn man
with dark hair, light olive skin, and green eyes appears on the
display. "This is T'Hale Marek of the Great House D'enekai—
one of the seven Great Ruling Houses of our world. I am

T'Hale of the Lower House of H'laeth, and have pledged our House to his."

"T'Hale? What does that mean?"

"It is a title of nobility. But in Marek's case, it is also one of royalty as well."

"Like a prince?" I ask.

He nods. "Yes. He is known as the Lonely Prince."

"Why?"

Vorek turns to me. "Prince Marek lost everything when our original home world—V'lorys—was destroyed. His parents made sure that everyone under the protection of their House was evacuated before them, before the destruction of V'lorys. Whereas the current Emperor and most of the other Great Houses evacuated their entire families first and their people later.

"Every V'loryn knows that Marek's parents gave up their seats on the last ship to two children that the Emperor's House had left behind. When word spread of his parents' noble sacrifice, more than three quarters of the Lower Houses pledged themselves to his." He pauses. "V'loryn families share a familial mental bond, similar to the al'nara. It is… not quite as strong as the al'nara, but it is the thread that links us to our parents and siblings. The loss of such a bond is devastating.

"To grow up without one, as Marek has done… I cannot imagine the loneliness of having no one. He was a child when his parents died, and he has lived all this time without the bond." He shakes his head. "If not for Tavek and my sister, I cannot imagine how terrible it would have been to be without this vital connection to another."

He continues. "No other Great House sacrificed as much as his for their people. He is a good and honorable male."

I study the man in the display, my heart sad for all that he lost. Despite his stoic expression, it is easy to read the pain behind his eyes in the image.

"That's terrible," I whisper. "What about your men? Are they still able to sense their families through the bond from here?"

Pain reflects behind his eyes. "No. Something about this world blocks not only our communications equipment, but the ability of my men to reach out to their families through the bond." He clenches his jaw. "It is why many of them worry that their families will believe they are dead. Fortunately, none of them are mated. If they had been, they and their bondmates could have died because of *L'talla*."

"What's L'talla?"

"Broken bond sickness. When we take a mate, we join them to us in the permanent mental bond of the S'acris. If one mate dies, the bond is broken, and the other usually follows in death shortly after."

He takes my hand. "There is something I must discuss with you, my Alana."

The way he says this makes me worry. "What is it?"

His wrist communicator chirps, and when he taps it, a man's voice comes across the speaker. "They've found someone."

"Who?"

"One of the Aerilon found a Terran male. They report he's wounded but alive. They are almost here."

Hope flares in my chest at the knowledge that another Terran has been found. I think of all the others, praying that they have somehow escaped the A'kai and are out there waiting for rescue even now.

I wonder if this man might have seen anyone else... one of my friends.

Vorek and I rush outside just as they land. Everyone is

gathered around them, but I push through the small crowd of people, eager to greet another Terran.

My heart stutters and stops when Harry's green eyes meet mine.

A beaming smile curves my mouth and I race toward him. "Harry!" I wrap my arms around him, hugging him close.

"Alana," he barely manages, holding me so tight I can barely breathe. His eyes fill with tears. "I was so worried you were dead. Thank god you're alive."

He gathers me in his arms, spinning me around. He's so pale and gaunt. I'm worried he's going to hurt himself.

CHAPTER 23

VOREK

My possessive instincts flare brightly as the Terran male gathers Alana in his arms. This must be the male she spoke of—and the way he is touching her I suspect he may have been her betrothed.

A low growl rumbles my chest as I level a dark glare at him. How dare he touch her? She is mine.

He spins her around and she begins kicking out her legs. "Put me down!" she calls out.

Instead of doing as she demands, he laughs.

I wrap my arms around her, and pull her away from him. I place myself protectively in front of her. I bare my fangs as possessive anger floods my veins. "She told you to put her down," I snarl. "I will end you for daring to touch her."

All the color drains from his face.

Her small hand on my back, draws my attention. "Vorek, it's all right. Harry wasn't trying to hurt me."

Confused, I narrow my eyes at Harry before shifting my

167

gaze back to Alana. "I thought he was holding you against your will."

"Holding her against her will?" Harry says incredulously. "I would never do that."

And yet, he did. I witnessed it mere moments ago.

She takes my hand. "I was just afraid he'd hurt himself holding me up like that. He wasn't holding me against my will. This is how Terrans sometimes greet each other, Vorek."

Her species are very tactile, this much I know. They both stare up at me expectantly.

"I apologize," I tell them. "It was a... misunderstanding." One that could have easily led to Harry's death because I was moments away from tearing him apart for touching her.

Al'iro's golden eyes meet mine full of concern. No doubt he understands just how close Harry was to certain death.

Al'iro directs them to take him to the med bay, and I follow closely, observing Alana closely as she interacts with this male.

Why she would desire him is beyond me. He is smaller than my people and obviously much weaker. He cannot possibly hope to keep her safe and provide for her on this hostile planet, especially since their species lack any form of natural defenses.

As Al'iro and another Healer place him in the MRU, Alana asks anxiously. "How is he?"

Al'iro shakes his head. "He has several fractures that are not fully healed. I will need to sedate him for the MRU to work efficiently."

As Al'iro explains this to Harry, she turns to me.

"This is Harry?" I gesture to him. "The male you spoke of?"

"Yes." She smiles and it is as if a sharpened blade has been speared through my heart. "I can't believe it. I'm so glad he's alive. I was so afraid he was dead."

Fierce possessiveness fills me as I stare down at her. I want nothing more than to pull her into my arms and carry her back to my quarters and claim her as my mate. My gaze drifts to the curve of her neck and shoulder and lands on the pulsing artery along her neck.

My fangs extend with want to sink them deep into her flesh and seal her to me in the sacred blood ritual of the S'acris. She is mine. Not his. She is my Si'an T'kara.

The halo of light that shines brightly around her head feels now as if it is only there to mock me. She is my Si'an T'kara, but she cannot be mine. A deep ache settles in my chest as I look to Harry. She has already made her choice.

I turn my gaze to her again. If I could get her alone, I could form the al'nara with her... attempt to manipulate her mind to choose me; to feel for me as I do her. Perhaps I could convince her to never leave me...

Curling my fingers into my palms, my claws extend and pierce my skin as I focus on the pain, struggling to bind the darkness within me. To manipulate the mind of another is the most heinous of crimes among my people, punishable by death.

She is my Si'an T'kara. Her blue eyes stare up at me, full of confusion. "Vorek, what's wrong?"

Consumed with guilt and shame, I imagine falling to my knees before her and begging her forgiveness that I would even consider such a terrible thing. After all that she has been through, how could this thought have ever crossed my mind?

Clenching my jaw as the reality of the situation comes into sharp focus, I force an impassive mask to my face. "I must go."

Without waiting for her response, I leave and head straight for my quarters. I must lock myself away before I do something I will regret. Already, I can feel my controls being stripped away as my mating cycle takes hold.

CHAPTER 24

ALANA

"Vorek, wait!" I start to go after him, but Al'iro's hand on my shoulder stops me.

"Leave him," he says. "I will go speak with him. Tend to your mate."

My mate? I follow his line of sight and realize he's talking about Harry. Before I can correct him, he rushes down the hallway after Vorek.

Tavek looks to me, his eyes full of concern despite his impassive expression. "It will be all right. Stay here. I will go see to my brother."

He leaves and I'm about to follow him when one of the other Aerilon Healers calls out to me.

I turn back to Harry. He's unconscious in the MRU. As I study his face, I observe how thin and pale he is. I can only imagine what he must have gone through.

I pull a chair up to his MRU and sit beside him, placing my hand on the glass. "You're safe now, Harry," I whisper, despite knowing he cannot hear me. "I can't wait to talk to you again."

CHAPTER 25

VOREK

Devastation washes through me as I leave the med bay. A dull ache throbs in my chest. The pain is so great, it threatens to overwhelm me, and I lean against the side wall as a maelstrom of emotions churns deep inside.

Al'iro claps a hand on my shoulder. "Vorek, are you all right?"

"I… do not know," I barely manage to reply. "Is this the mating cycle or *L'talla*?"

His eyes widen. "Broken bond sickness? How could you have this? You did not seal her to you yet."

"I… do not know," I reply. "I joined with her mind in the al'nara. Perhaps that was enough of a connection to—"

"Vorek?" Tavek's voice calls out behind us. "What's wrong?"

He rushes toward me and stops, blinking several times as he regards me.

JESSICA GRAYSON & ARIA WINTER

Al'iro turns to him. "Can your people suffer from L'talla without sealing the bond?"

Tavek inhales sharply. "L'talla? I... she is a different species. No V'loryn has ever taken a mate outside of our race." He grips my shoulders. "You did not seal her to you."

"No, but we shared our minds in the al'nara."

He clenches his jaw. "It is forbidden to do that until you are bonded. You know the risks of—"

"I do, but... the first time it happened was an accident. I was unconscious. The next time... she had already agreed to be mine. I thought it was safe."

Tavek turns to Al'iro. "You must do something. You cannot let my brother die from L'talla."

Al'iro frowns. "I thought L'talla only happened when one's mate died."

"It can occur if the mate bond is broken for any reason," Tavek explains. "Our people mate for life. L'talla is the reason we do not mate outside of our species."

Al'iro runs the scanner over me and lifts a worried gaze to mine. "From what I studied of your medical library, your readings do not match L'talla. But, they do indicate something else."

"What is it?"

He places a hand on my shoulder, his golden eyes searching mine. "Your hormone levels are elevated. It has to be related to your mating cycle."

I curl my hands into fists at my side, frustrated that I had not recognized the signs of it worsening sooner.

Tavek's eyes flash with concern.

"I must seclude myself," I look to Al'iro. "I need you to seal off my quarters so that I cannot leave them."

His brow furrows deeply. "Why?"

"I have formed the al'nara with her. Her mind, her scent, the feel of her skin beneath my fingers, and her body against

174

mine... All of this is already imprinted upon me. Although we are not bonded, my body already instinctively craves hers as my mate. The only way to keep her safe is to seal me in here so that I cannot search for her."

"Are you certain she is with the Terran male?" Al'iro asks.

"Even if she wasn't, I could not bind her to me like this. Not in my current condition. Certainly not while I'm in the throes of my mating cycle. You've scanned her. You know how fragile her people are compared to mine. I could hurt her, Al'iro." I meet his golden eyes evenly. "Just tell her that I need to rest. She has already been through much and I will not have her burdened with this as well."

Al'iro places a hand on my shoulder. "Fine. I will seal you in your quarters. She will be safe. My vow."

Tavek casts a worried glance at me before leaving with Al'iro.

As they leave, I sit down on the edge of the bed and fall back on the comforter. I close my eyes, and an image of Alana smiling at me appears in my mind.

I understand now why love is such a dangerous emotion. Sadness wars with anger as my thoughts turn to Harry. I want to challenge him—make him prove himself, prove to me he can protect and defend her from all harm.

Savage and murderous thoughts run through my mind as I think on this pathetic Terran male, but I force myself to push them down.

If he is her choice, I must honor it.

I cannot force her to be mine.

Sadness and despair fill me anew, and I close my eyes against the pain, sending a desperate prayer to the goddess asking her to take this terrible ache from my chest. I do not want it, and I can hardly bear to think of Alana belonging to someone else.

Devastation gives way to possessive anger. My fangs lengthen with want to claim her.

She is mine, and I am hers.

CHAPTER 26

ALANA

Al'iro comes back into the med bay, and I walk over to him. "Is Vorek all right?"

He shakes his head. "He is ill and has retired to his quarters."

Worry spikes through me. "What's wrong with him? What kind of illness is it? Take me to him. I—I need to see him. He needs someone to take care of him."

Al'iro sighs heavily. "Is the Terran your mate?"

My head jerks back. "What?"

Tavek moves to my side, a hint of irritation shifting into his gaze. "Is he yours?" He gestures to Harry, lying unconscious in the MRU.

I frown. "Why are you asking me this. I'm with Vorek."

"Are you?" Tavek arches a brow.

"Yes," I state firmly, irritated he would question me like this. "Harry is just my friend. Nothing more." I meet his gaze evenly. "Besides, what right do you have to question me like this? My relationship with Vorek is—"

"Forgive me," Tavek says quickly. "I merely worry for my brother. He was... devastated. He thought you were with Harry."

"He thought he was experiencing L'talla because of it," Al'iro adds."

L'talla. I remember Vorek explaining this to me. Worry tightens my chest. "I don't understand. Why would he have this? We haven't bonded yet."

Al'iro sighs. "Vorek thought because he had already linked with you in the al'nara that—"

I look to Tavek as the realization hits me. "Your people can die from this, right? From L'talla?"

"Yes. It is an excruciating death."

My heart stops as I think back on the way Vorek looked at me before he left. That was pain that flashed behind his eyes. I'm sure of it. I hate that he thinks I'm with someone else. I start for the hallway to head to his quarters.

"Where are you going?"

"I have to speak with him. I have to explain."

"You cannot go to him," Al'iro says, stopping me abruptly. "I sealed off his quarters. He needs to rest."

"Rest?" I ask incredulously. "How can you just leave him like that when he might have L'talla?"

"Trust us," Tavek says. "He is fine. He merely needs a few days to recover."

I turn to Al'iro. His eyes dart to Tavek and something unspoken passes between them. "Vorek will be fine, Alana. He asked to be left alone during this time."

"I don't understand. Why?"

Again, they exchange a glance, and I realize that I'm not going to get an answer. "You must trust us," Al'iro says. "All will be well in a few days."

Tears sting my eyes as I step out into the hallway. I should have realized something was wrong by the way he looked at me after Harry arrived.

"Where are you going?" Tavek calls out.

"Outside to get some fresh air," I lie.

As I head toward Vorek's quarters, I'm desperate to speak with him, wanting to explain to him that Harry is just my friend. I hate that he thinks I don't love him.

How could I not have even considered he might misunderstand?

When I reach the spot where I remember the door being, I place my hand on the wall searching for the panel I cannot see.

Frustration burns through me as I keep hitting the wall, but nothing happens. Desperate, I pound on it. "Vorek! Vorek!"

The outline of the door lights along the wall, as I find the spot for my hand. As soon as it opens, I see Vorek standing just inside.

His glowing green eyes study mine, swirling with black. "You should not be here," he says in a low voice. "You need to leave."

"Why?"

"It is not safe."

I cup his cheek. "What's wrong? Al'iro said you thought you were going through L'talla, Vorek. But I had to see you, to explain. Harry isn't my mate. He's my friend. I only want you, Vorek. No one else."

A low growl rumbles his chest, and he clenches his jaw. "You need to leave," his voice is rough as he speaks. "Now, Alana."

"Why? I don't understand."

"I am not experiencing L'talla. I thought that was what this was, but I was wrong. It is my mating cycle."

"Mating cycle? What does that mean?"

His eyes turn feral, obsidian black as his gaze holds mine.

"Between the ages of twenty-eight and thirty-five cycles, our biology compels us to find a mate, to form the S'acris."

"I don't understand. I thought you wanted me as your mate. Was I wrong?"

"No," he says darkly. "I desire to claim you more than anything, but I fear I will hurt you."

"Why?"

"During our mating cycle, it is difficult to maintain… control. It is three to five days of repeated matings. If I take you now and seal you to me, I do not know how much control I will have. I could hurt you, Alana."

"I trust you, Vorek," I whisper softly. "You won't hurt me."

"Please, Alana." His hand trembles as he touches my cheek. "You must leave now, while you still can."

"No." I stretch up on my toes and wrap my arms around his neck, crushing my lips to his.

At first, he doesn't move, but after a moment, he slips his arms around me and pulls me close, returning my kiss with equal fervor.

"Vorek," I breathe between kisses. "I love you."

"Alana," he breathes my name out like a sigh.

I curl my tongue around his, and he lifts me into his arms, pressing my back against the wall as his mouth meshes repeatedly with mine.

"I only want you," I whisper against his lips. "No one else."

He kisses me long and deep, stealing the breath from my lungs.

When he pulls back, I'm breathless and panting. I touch his face, tracing the sharp line of his brow as I stare deep into his eyes. "I want you, Vorek. I want to be yours, my love."

He cups my cheek, pain etched in his normally stoic features. "Goddess, help me, I cannot push you away."

"Then… don't," I breathe.

He drops his forehead to mine. "You do not know what you are saying," he rasps.

"I want you, Vorek. Bind me to you, my love."

Something inside him snaps. He seals his mouth over mine in a searing kiss and carries me to the bed. Gently, he lays me down beneath the comforter, then crawls over me. He unties the belt from my waist and tears off my clothing before removing his as well.

His gaze holds mine as he runs his hand lightly down my bare skin, staring at me in reverence. "You are perfect, Alana," he whispers.

I reach up, tracing my fingers over the muscular planes of his abdomen and chest—pure, masculine perfection.

My eyes drop to his length, hard and erect, a bead of liquid gathering on the end. I carefully brush my thumb over the tip. His eyes swirl from glowing green to obsidian as I mark my abdomen with his essence.

His nostrils flare as his fangs extend, and I realize it is taking every bit of his control to remain still. "You are mine," he growls.

He kisses me long and deep before pressing a series of suctioning kisses down the length of my body. When he drags his tongue through my folds, I arch up against him as he concentrates on the small bundle of nerves at the apex.

He growls low in his throat, and the vibration moves straight through me, sending ripples of pleasure straight to my core.

He takes my hand, threading his fingers through mine. The connection flares brightly between us, and I moan as desire pulses strongly across the link.

Something dark and primal uncoils from deep within him, clawing beneath the surface of his mind, desperate to break through and claim me as his mate. I can feel his struggle to hold it back, afraid that he will scare me.

"I want all of you, Vorek. I'm not afraid," I whisper. "I trust you. Completely."

A low growl of arousal escapes his throat as he continues to tease his tongue around the softly hooded flesh between my thighs, my entire body goes taut like a bowstring, and then I'm coming harder than I ever have before.

I'm breathless and panting as he moves up my body. I gasp as the crown of his length bumps against my entrance. The breath stutters from my lungs as he pushes into me. Everything is tight and uncomfortable at first as my body stretches around his length.

He stops, his expression full of worry. "I do not want to hurt you."

I cup his cheek. "I'll be fine. I just need a moment to adjust."

My body slowly relaxes around him, and he begins to advance once more.

I moan as he rocks his hips back and forth until he's fully seated inside me.

"So tight," he rasps.

Through the touch of our skin, I can sense he's on the razor-sharp edge of his control, struggling to hold back for fear he will hurt me.

"I trust you, Vorek." I cup his cheek. "Seal me to you, my love."

He presses his mouth to my own, curling his tongue around mine and deepening our kiss. He groans as I wrap my legs tighter around him, then rips his mouth from mine and sinks his fangs deep into my neck.

His mind pours into mine like liquid pouring into a glass as we fall deep into the al'nara. *"You are mine, and I am yours."*

"I am yours, and you are mine."

We swim through the ocean of our combined thoughts, and as he begins to stroke inside me, my pleasure heightens at the experience of every sensation as he moves deep in my channel.

He growls in arousal as he experiences my pleasure, the sensations moving between us in a feedback loop driving my desire even higher, and I'm lost in overwhelming pleasure.

As I feel the gentle pull on my skin as he drinks of my blood, I hold him close, threading my fingers through his hair.

"Intoxicating," he breathes against my skin as he pulls away. He swipes his tongue over the two puncture wounds and seals them. "You are mine, Alana."

The ridges of his length create the most delicious friction, and my toes curl with pleasure as each stroke into my body becomes longer, deeper, and more forceful.

He drops down low, wrapping his arms around my waist and holding me so close there is no space between our bodies.

"Mine," he groans as he thrusts deep within me.

I trace my hands down his back, feeling the powerful muscles with each thrust as he claims me completely.

I gasp as everything becomes tighter somehow, almost to the point of pain, but not quite. It expands into intense pleasure that steals the breath from my lungs. "What's happening?" I barely manage.

"My knot is expanding," he grits through his teeth. "Goddess, you feel so good," he growls.

A low moan escapes me. "I didn't know you—"

I start to say 'knot' but stop as my mouth falls open, and my entire body locks up a moment before I fall over the edge. His gaze holds mine as overwhelming pleasure washes over and through me, and I cry out his name.

"Mine!" He roars above me, his length pulsing strongly as he fills me with the delicious warmth of his seed. It feels as though it goes on forever. And just when I'm starting to come down from my orgasm, he takes my hands in his, pinning them to the mattress beside me as he strengthens our connection.

I gasp, then cry out his name as his length pulses again, and he erupts deep inside me, my body clenching around him, pulling his seed deep into my womb.

I'm breathless and panting as he rolls us onto our sides, his length still knotted deep in my channel. He tenderly brushes the hair back from my face as I blink several times, fighting against my fatigue as my body lies spent beside his.

He seals his mouth over mine in a claiming kiss, then begins to move deep inside me again. I pull back just enough to meet his gaze. "You want me again so soon?"

"Yes," he breathes. "I need you."

He rolls me beneath him, and my lips part in a low moan as he begins to stroke inside me once more.

CHAPTER 27

ALANA

When I wake the next morning, I'm wrapped up in Vorek's arms. I turn to face him, wincing slightly at the dull ache between my thighs, reminding me I've been thoroughly claimed by my V'loryn bondmate.

He skims the tip of his nose alongside mine, then presses a tender kiss to my lips. I run my fingers through the hairs at the nape of his neck.

He pulls back to regard me, his eyes drifting down to the mark he gave me. "Can you feel my presence in the back of your mind, my Alana?"

The gentle hum of his consciousness fills me with warmth as he sends a wave of love along the tethered bond between us. "Yes, my love," I whisper. "I can."

I reach up and trace his lips, marveling at the perfection of his mouth. "I love you, Vorek."

He pulls me closer to him, and I wince slightly.

He glances down at me. "Did I hurt you?"

"I'm fine, my love. Just a bit sore. I've heard it's normal for the first time."

He drops his forehead to mine. "I should have been more careful with you. I—"

I press a finger to his lips to silence him. "It's all right, Vorek. Trust me. I'm fine."

He nods, and then stands from the bed.

I marvel at the perfection of his body. The thick corded muscles flex as he scoops me into his arms and carries me to the cleansing room. We stand beneath the shower, and then he wraps one of the fur cloaks around both of us.

"It is tradition to greet the dawn the morning after our first joining," he says. "It symbolizes the beginning of our lives together, as one."

"That sounds beautiful, my love." He settles me in his lap as we sit before the viewscreen, staring out at the snowy landscape beyond.

I relax back against the solid warmth of his chest as we watch the first yellow-orange rays of the sun rise over the snow-capped mountains in the distance.

As the sun peaks above the mountain range, he cups my chin and turns my head back to his, brushing his lips against mine in a tender kiss.

I turn in his arms to face him, straddling his hips.

Wrapping my hand around his l'ok, I position him at my entrance. He groans as I lower myself onto him until he's fully seated deep inside me. His gaze holds mine intently as he begins to move his hips against mine. "You are mine," he whispers. "And I am yours."

CHAPTER 28

VOREK

My wrist comm chirps loudly, and I quickly press the button, hoping it will not awaken my Si'an T'kara beside me.

Tavek's face appears on the screen, his expression impassive but his eyes full of worry. It is unnerving to see my brother this way. It takes much to disturb his calm.

"What is wrong?"

"A Mosauran flew over our shields. It was Rokan— Commander Markus's second in command. He scented Alana. One of the Aerilon—Ol'naro—went to speak with him, and he demanded to speak with her."

I bristle. "No."

"That is what he told him. He refuses to leave without speaking to you."

"I will be there shortly."

I glance at my Si'an T'kara, still asleep in the bed. Carefully, I stand and then tuck the comforter around her shoulders to keep her warm. I dress quickly and then quietly leave the room.

Anger floods my veins and my protective instincts flare as I step outside and find Rokan on the other side of our shield. I am still deep in the throes of my mating cycle and the mere sight of him makes me want to tear out his throat.

He is in his two-legged form. The green coloring of his cheeks darkens, standing out in sharp contrast to the rest of his silver-white scales. His green eyes lock onto mine, his vertically slit pupils contracting. "You have a Terran female, do you not?"

I narrow my eyes. "Yes."

"I wish to speak with her."

"No," I state firmly.

He narrows his eyes. "Why not?"

"She is mine," I growl low in my throat. "I will not risk her."

His nostrils flare. "I would never harm a female."

"Even so," I grind out. "Your people are volatile and aggressive. I will not risk—"

"Lies that your kind spread about mine," he snarls. "I demand that you allow me to speak with her. Now."

My nails extend into lethal claws as I bare my fangs in aggression. "Leave now, while you still can, Rokan."

"Not until I am allowed to see her."

"She. Is. Mine," I growl.

His eyes go wide. "Since when do your people take a mate outside of your species?"

"She is my Si'an T'kara—my fated one. I will not allow you near Alana. You or any of your kind. You will not take her from me."

"I have not come to—"

"Leave!" I snarl. "Or I will end you."

"Fine," he states. "But we will be back."

Without warning, he spreads his silver-white wings out behind him and takes off into the sky.

I look to Tavek. "Double the patrols of our territory. We cannot take any chances. The Mosaurans may return with more people next time and we need to be ready."

He dips his chin in a subtle nod and I return to my quarters. My protective instincts flaring as I make my way back to Alana, desperate to hold her in my arms again.

When I reach her, she is already awake. "Where did you go?"

I sit on the edge of the bed and take her hand. Reluctantly, I explain what happened with Rokan.

"Markus is the one who has my friend, right?" she asks.

"Yes."

Her eyes are full of worry. "Why do they want to take me? Why not just bring her here? Or invite us to see them? Why demand you hand me over?"

With a slight clench of my jaw, I meet her gaze evenly. "I know Markus, but much has happened between us and their people. He cannot help what he is: volatile, aggressive to any who are not Mosauran."

"What about Lara?" her eyes flash with worry, and I realize I've said the wrong thing.

I move quickly to reassure her. "He would never harm her. They do not take slaves, and they cherish their females. This I know is truth. She is safe with them. But, you... I will not hand you over to them. I believe they would try to take you from me. Keep you."

"But why?"

"They do not trust us... and we do not entirely trust them."

"It is only a matter of time before they come back," she

says, worry evident in her tone. "What if they try to take me?"

I wrap a possessive arm around my bondmate. "Then, we will be ready for them when they do."

CHAPTER 29

ALANA

When I wake in the morning, Vorek's arms are wrapped around me, holding me close to his chest. He took me several times last night, his fiercely possessive instincts demanding that he fill me with his seed, marking me with his scent so that all other males will know I am his.

He told me his people are possessive and protective of their mates. Through our bond, I could feel his worry that the Mosaurans will try to take me from him and his rage that they would dare even think to touch me.

He is V'loryn, and this is their nature. Through our bond, I understand this part of him, and I embrace it completely. Even during the height of his mating cycle, he never hurt me. And he never did anything I did not want.

Anytime he even thought I might be uncomfortable, he would stop and ask me if I was all right.

He gently nuzzles my hair. I turn in his arms to face him.

"Good morning, my love." I lean forward and press a tender kiss to his lips.

In the back of my mind, I can sense his presence. The intense fire that burned so brightly within him during his mating cycle is now burned down to mere embers. I'm not sure if it's been three days or five. We made love so many times I'm not sure how long we've been here in his quarters.

I shift in his arms to pull him closer. The dull ache between my thighs fills me with warmth at the remembrance of his body joined with mine, reminding me that I've been thoroughly claimed by my V'loryn bondmate.

Having sensed my slight discomfort, his eyes flash with worry and he pulls back the comforter. Guilt and distress bleed across the bond at the darkening bruise on my hip in the shape of his handprint. "I must be more careful with you, Alana."

I take his hand in mine. "Search my thoughts, Vorek. You'll see that I'm fine, my love."

I open my mind to him, showing him how much I enjoyed making love to him and how much I want him still. The memory of what we did over the past few days makes desire pool deep in my core.

He closes his eyes a moment and when he opens them again their glowing green color swirls with black. His nostrils flare. "I can scent your need, Alana."

I brush my lips to his. He opens his mouth and curls his tongue around mine, deepening our kiss. "You want me again so soon?" he whispers, and I can sense his wonder at this through the bond.

"Yes, my love."

He rolls me beneath him and enters me in one long stroke as his mind pours into mine like liquid pouring into a glass. His voice echoes deep within as he whispers my name in awe-filled reverence. *"Alana, you are mine, and I am yours."*

~

When we finally leave Vorek's quarters, his brother Tavek seeks us out right away. I remember how Vorek told me they have the familial bond between them, so I suppose that's how he knew to find us now.

As he speaks with Vorek, my thoughts keep turning to Lara and the others. Another Mosauran came while Vorek and I were locked in his quarters for the past few days. Commander Markus—Lara's mate—sent him to try to retrieve me.

Tavek's eyes flash with concern as he looks between me and Vorek. "When we sent the Mosauran away, he said that Commander Markus would be the one who will come here next. I suspect he will come soon. He wants to speak with you about the Terrans. And he wants you to give Alana over to his people."

"I don't understand," I tell Vorek. "Why do they want to take me away?"

He shakes his head. "Perhaps it is because of the history of deep mistrust between our two races. I do not believe they would harm you. But I do believe they would try to keep you from me."

"But why?"

"Despite that our cultures are very different, our anatomy and our... abilities are similar to the A'kai. Markus once confided in me that his people are concerned that mine could turn back to the path our ancestors used to follow. The same one the A'kai follow now."

A small shiver runs through me at the memory of all I went through when I was their slave. As I lift my gaze to Vorek, I know without a doubt that he could never be like them. I take his hand in mine. "You are nothing like them, Vorek."

His lips quirk up at the edges in his barely-there smile as he sends a wave of love and affection across the bond, filling my chest with warmth.

Tavek turns to us. "Harry is in the med bay with Al'iro. He is anxious to speak with you."

Vorek walks with me to the med bay to check on Harry. I can hardly wait to talk to him too. And I'm desperate to ask if he knows anything about the other women. Maybe he knows what happened to some of them. I didn't get a chance to ask him before.

When we reach the med bay, Harry is in the MRU and Al'iro is standing over him.

"He asked me to remove his tracker that had been placed by the A'kai. He's still unconscious," Al'iro says as we enter. "But, he is doing well and should awaken soon."

"Thank you, Al'iro."

He looks between me and Vorek. "Congratulations on your bonding."

"Thank you," I reply, my cheeks warming slightly.

Vorek's wristband chirps, and he sighs heavily, glancing down at the display. "I must go. We are sending more people out to search for the others."

I stretch up on my toes and press a tender kiss to his lips. "I'm going to stay here. Al'iro can start my lessons while I wait for Harry to wake up. Maybe he knows where some of the others are."

Vorek looks to Al'iro, then back to me, and nods. "When he wakes, contact me. I'd also like to speak to him. He might be able to lead us to some of your people."

I squeeze his hand gently, reluctant to let him go, before he steps out into the hallway.

When I turn back to Al'iro, his gaze drifts to Harry. "We will continue to search for your people and will not give up until we find them, Alana. We will not abandon them to the A'kai."

His voice is thick with emotion, and I blink back tears at the memory of what Vorek told me of Al'iro's sister.

He lowers his gaze. "My sister was held my them. She—" his voice catches. He draws in a deep breath and clenches his jaw.

"Vorek told me what happened," I murmur. "I'm so sorry for your loss."

He lifts tear-filled eyes to mine. "I am glad you are here and that you are a Healer, Alana. You understand what your people have been through. I believe such knowledge will help us to not lose anyone to the darkness"—his voice quavers —"like my sister. Do you understand?"

"Yes, I do. We will work together."

He gives me a pained smile, then hands me a tablet. "Let us get you as familiar as possible with everything before more of your people arrive."

I take the tablet and listen carefully as he begins explaining the various symbols to me and how to use the medical equipment they have on hand.

Some of this, I can memorize, but it's easy to see I will have to study V'loryn and Aerilon as I learn. The translator works for speech, but until Terran Standard is programmed into the chips, it will not help us with the written word, unfortunately.

Still, there are many things I'm able to do in the meantime.

I get so lost in my studies that when Harry's MRU beeps to alert us that he is awake, I almost miss it.

Al'iro and I rush to his bed, and when his eyes snap open. As the casing retracts, he sits up and gives me a tight hug. "Alana, I was so worried about you." He levels an angry glare at Al'iro. "When I woke up, they told me you were with Vorek, but they wouldn't let me see you or talk to you."

"It's all right, Harry. I'm fine."

"What happened to you?" He pulls back, his eyes searching mine. "Where were you?"

"Vorek and I—" I pause, unsure how to explain. Finally, I decide on, "We sort of got married."

I sense Vorek's presence in the back of my mind before he even steps into the room. When I turn and find him at the door, I smile brightly.

"I felt something through the bond," he says. "Is Harry—"

He stops as soon as his gaze lands on my friend.

"Harry"—I gesture to Vorek—"this is Vorek. My husband —bondmate," I correct.

Harry's jaw drops. "You married an alien?"

"Yes." I smile brightly. "A very handsome one, don't you agree?" I take Vorek's hand, and feel the swell of pride filling him at my words.

He frowns. "Why didn't you say anything? You just up and disappeared for the past few days and I—"

"It's complicated," I tell him.

Harry regards Vorek with narrowed eyes. "First things first."

Vorek's brow furrows. "What is it?"

"Alana is my best friend. If you ever hurt her or break her heart, I don't care who you are, I will end you."

Vorek gives him a solemn nod. "I will cherish her until I draw my last breath. I swear it to the stars. My vow."

A smile curves Harry's mouth as he winks at me and gestures a thumb at Vorek. "I like him. I think he's definitely a keeper. Does he have any friends you can introduce me to?" he teases.

I laugh and Vorek arches a brow. I'm glad Harry still has

his sense of humor. At least some of who he was survived all the horrible things we've been through.

Vorek regards him a moment before asking. "You have a preference for males?"

"Yes, I do," Harry huffs. "What? You don't have any same sex couples among your people?"

"Of course, we do," Vorek implies incredulously.

"Then... what's with the look and the question?"

Vorek slips his arm around my waist, tugging me into his side. "I thought you might be a rival for my Si'an T'kara's affections. But I am pleased to find that I was wrong."

Harry rolls his eyes. "Oh, please. Alana is my best friend. She's like a sister to me. So that makes you my new brother-in-law," he teases.

Vorek's relief is easily palpable through the bond. I turn to him and cup his cheek. "You have nothing to worry about, my love. I'm all yours."

Tenderly, he nuzzles my hair and his tr'llen purr sounds low in his chest. "Good," he whispers against the shell of my ear.

I turn back to Harry. "Did you see any others while you were... out there?"

"Yes." His expression hardens as he darts a glance at Al'iro. "I keep telling him I want to go back out and search, but he insists I'm not well enough yet."

Ignoring his obvious irritation, Vorek asks, "How many did you see?"

"Three. And they weren't alone." he says, the tone of his voice filling me with dread. "One of them was with some guy that can shift into this huge wolf-like creature."

"Lycaons," I tell him. "That's what they're called. They chased us here."

"Lycaons," he repeats the word, committing it to memory. "And I saw two others with the A'kai." He looks to Vorek.

"Please. I appreciate the rescue, but I have to get back out there. We need to rescue the others."

"Our people are already searching," Vorek replies. "If you go with them, you can help guide them to the areas where you remember seeing the others. We'll give you a blaster and assign you to someone to search with."

"Thank you. That's all I ask. To be able to search for the rest of my people," Harry says.

I turn to my bondmate. "I need to speak with Lara. Maybe if she comes with her mate, we can talk things out and figure out a plan to work together to find the rest of our people."

Vorek's worry travels along the bond. "I will reach out to them. But you will stay behind the shield when they come."

"All right," I agree.

CHAPTER 30

ALANA

A deafening roar splits the air and my heart stutters and stops. The Mosaurans must be here. They've finally come, and I can hardly wait to see Lara. My eyes are wide as I turn to Vorek. "Stay here, Alana. It's the Mosaurans. We're expecting Commander Markus."

Before I can say anything, he races from the room and out into the hallway. Harry and I follow after him, ignoring Al'iro's protests that we stay.

As soon as we reach the main entrance and glance out the airlock, my jaw drops. An enormous dragon hovers in the air just above the defense shield.

Silver scales shimmer iridescent beneath the sunlight, wings billowing out like great sails on a ship. Violet eyes stare down at Vorek and the others menacingly as he bellows another roar of challenge.

He circles and lands just on the other side of the clear barrier, and I gasp as he shifts forms into something similar to a man, but not quite. He's just as tall as the V'loryns and the Aerilon, and he is covered in silver scales. Two cranial ridges extend from his forehead like a *V*, disappearing into his dark hairline.

He's completely nude, but where male anatomy would be, I notice only a line in his scales. His feet and hands are tipped with lethal, black claws, and when he opens his mouth, he reveals two rows of gleaming, white fangs.

"Markus," Vorek addresses him.

"Vorek," he replies. "As agreed, I have come to let Lara speak with Alana. I'll call for Rokan once I have your vow she will be safe—that you will not try to take her from me."

A menacing growl rumbles deep in Vorek's chest. "You have my vow."

Markus narrows his eyes. "And if you dare try to deceive me and take *my* mate, I will end you, Vorek."

"My people honor our vows, Markus," Vorek snaps. "I cannot believe you are threatening me, especially when you are responsible for us all being here in the first place."

"Markus?" I step out of the hatch and move to Vorek's side, but he grips my forearm, pulling me protectively behind him.

Markus's violet eyes study me a moment, and he snarls. "Let go of her, Vorek. If she wants to come with us, you must let her. If you do not, I will find a way to destroy your shield and your ship. My vow."

Vorek's nails extend into sharpened claws, and his eyes turn obsidian black as his fangs extend. "If you dare try to take her from me, I will end you," he grits through his teeth. "My vow."

The other V'loryns appear just as fearsome, and as I glance at the Aerilon, I notice their fangs and claws extended, as well. I would be afraid if I did not already trust them.

"Do you have my friend? Lara?"

Markus straightens. "Yes. She is my mate. If you come with us, we will protect you."

I shake my head. "I'm not in any danger here. Vorek is my bondmate. You already know this. I love him."

Markus blinks several times, then narrows his eyes at Vorek. "Since when do V'loryns take mates outside of their race?"

Vorek arches a brow, his stance relaxing a bit, eyes swirling from black to their normal glowing green. "I could ask the same of you."

"Where's Lara? Please. I want to see her. She's like a sister to me."

Markus hesitates a moment, then shifts back into his dragon form. He releases a bellowing roar, and I gasp as another sounds back in return.

Vorek wraps a protective arm around my waist as another dragon flies toward us from the mountain. My hands fly to my face on a gasp when I notice the rider on its back is Lara.

My heart flutters with unbridled excitement and relief at seeing my friend. When the dragon lands, his emerald-green eyes study us warily before kneeling to allow her to slide off his back.

He shifts forms, and so does Markus.

I watch as Lara runs to Markus's arms, and he wraps her up in a protective embrace.

"Lara?"

Her head whips toward me, and she flashes a beaming smile. "Alana!"

I break into a run, racing toward the barrier, and Lara does the same. Vorek's voice calls out behind me, ordering it lowered before we reach it.

As soon as it drops, we practically barrel into each other,

embracing warmly. Tears spill down my cheeks as I hug her tight. "Lara, I'm so glad you're alive! I was so worried."

"Me too, Alana."

Harry races toward us and hugs us both. "Thank god you're all right, Lara. We were so worried about you."

A low rumble sounds nearby, and I pull back to see Markus standing behind Lara and Vorek behind me, eyeing each other with an icy glare. Vorek's lips are pulled back in a feral snarl, baring his fangs.

"Stop it!" I snap at them both. "You don't need to fight. We're all on the same side."

Both of them blink at me. Vorek cocks his head to the side. "They are Mosaurans. They are volatile and aggressive and—"

"I'm sure they have problems with you, too," I counter. "But, can we at least agree that neither of you means us any harm?"

Markus curls his arm around Lara's waist and gently nuzzles her temple. "On this, we are in agreement."

I take Vorek's hand, and he pulls me close to his side, wrapping a protective arm around me. "More of our people are still out there." I gesture toward the mountains and the icy landscape beyond. "We need to work together so we can find them."

Markus regards me curiously. "What are you suggesting?"

I tip my chin up. "An alliance. I'm not going to be kept from seeing my friend just because your people cannot get along. So, I suggest you learn how to work together."

A smile quirks the edge of Vorek's mouth, and his amusement bubbles across our bond.

Markus turns to Vorek. "They may be small, but what Terrans lack in size, they make up for in ferocity."

Vorek dips his chin in marked agreement.

EPILOGUE

ALANA

As I sit at my workstation, attempting to study three languages—V'loryn, Aerilon, and Mosauran—my eyes blink open and closed with the struggle to stay awake.

Warm hands on my shoulders are Vorek's as he approaches from behind me. "You are tired, my Si'an T'kara. You should rest."

"How can I? Most of my people are still missing, Vorek. I have to be ready to treat them when we find them." Tears fill my eyes. "If someone else comes in as injured and beaten as Violet, I need to be able to take care of them."

He nods, and his gaze drifts to the other room where Al'iro sits at his post next to Violet as she lies unconscious in the MRU. His wings, now glowing, are drooped behind him, observing her with a devastated expression on his face.

"She is his fated one," Vorek says softly. "The Aerilon— their wings only glow when they find them."

A tear slips down my cheek. "She's been through so much, Vorek."

"What do your scans tell you of her condition?"

A small shudder runs through me as I think of all of her injuries. "Her injuries were... severe, but Al'iro says the MRU will heal them. It will just take time. Several more hours, probably."

He gathers me in his arms and lifts me to his chest. "Come to bed, my Si'an T'kara. You need to rest."

Vorek carries me down the hallway to our quarters and gently lays me down upon the soft bedding.

He pulls at my clothing to remove it, then undresses himself, crawling into the bed beside me, holding me close.

I was tired only a moment ago, but being next to him like this... I'm fully awake, my entire body humming in awareness of him.

His nostrils flare, and his eyes swirl from glowing green to obsidian black. "I can scent your need, my Alana."

Cupping the back of his neck, I pull his mouth to mine. He captures my lips in a searing kiss, then rolls me beneath him.

He kisses a heated trail along my jaw and down my neck to the valley of my breasts, moving sensually down my body to lave his tongue over the soft peak. It turns into a sensitive, hardened bead beneath his attentions. I moan as he travels lower, already anticipating what will happen next.

He goes still, and I lift my head. "What's wrong?"

His nostrils flare as he scents my lower abdomen, and his eyes widen when they meet mine. "You are carrying our child," he whispers, his voice full of wonder.

"Are you sure? It's only been less than a month since—"

"I am certain. Your scent has changed." He places his open palm over my abdomen. "I can sense the lifespark of our child in your womb, Alana."

He takes my hand, and I smile as he transmits it to me through the al'nara. Tears fill my eyes and roll softly down my cheeks.

"Does this upset you?" he asks, his eyes full of worry.

"No," my voice quavers. "I just… didn't think it was possible between us."

"And now?"

I tug on his arm, pulling him back up so his face is level with mine. I cup his cheeks with both hands and press my lips softly to his, whispering against them. "I never knew it was possible to be this happy."

A smile quirks his lips as he captures my mouth in a claiming kiss, whispering in my mind. *"I love you beyond all reason and rational thought. I loved you before I even understood what love was, my Alana."*

When I wake during the night from a bad dream, his body is curled protectively around mine. I turn in his arms to face him and find him already awake.

He rests his forehead gently to mine as he smooths his hand across my back in a soothing gesture. "I am sorry I woke you," he whispers. "You were having a nightmare, Alana."

"What time is it?" I ask.

"It is still early. You should go back to sleep."

V'loryns don't require as much rest as Terrans. I know he often lays beside me for hours while he's awake simply because he loves holding me as I sleep. But sometimes he gets up and begins his day before I wake. But after experiencing my nightmare, I don't want him to leave. "Will you stay with me?"

He places his palm low over my abdomen, and his expression softens as his glowing green eyes stare deep into mine. "Always, my Si'an T'kara."

ALSO BY JESSICA GRAYSON

The next book in series is available here. *Al'iro and Violet's story:*
Rescued: Fae Alien Romance

If you're curious about the Kyo (the Kitsune) and his human mate
Anna, their story: **Rescued: Fox Shifter Romance**

If you're curious about the *"Marek—The Lonely Prince of V'lora"* and
his human mate, his story is already available. **Lost in the Deep End**
(Read the completed V'loryn Trilogy)

If you enjoyed this book, please leave a review on Amazon and/or
Goodreads. *Want more in this series ?*

Ice World Warrior Series

Claimed: Dragon Shifter Romance

Bound: Vampire Alien Romance

Rescued: Fae Alien Romance

Stolen: Werewolf Romance

Taken: Vampire Alien Romance

Fated: Dragon Shifter Romance

Protected: Dragon Shifter Romance

Do you like Elves and Vampires? I have a Vampire Alien Romance
series you might enjoy.

V'loryn Series (Vampire Alien Romance)

Lost in the Deep End

Beneath a Different Sky

Under a Silver Moon

Want Dragon Shifters? You can dive into their world with this completed Duology.

Mosauran Series (Dragon Shifter Alien Romance)

The Edge of it All

Shape of the Wind

Do you like Fairy Tale Retellings?

Fairy Tale Retellings (Once Upon a Fairy Tale Romance Series)

Taken by the Dragon: A Beauty and the Beast Retelling

Captivated by the Fae: A Cinderella Retelling

Rescued By The Merman: A Little Mermaid Retelling

Bound To The Elf Prince: A Snow White Retelling

Claimed By The Bear King: A Snow Queen Retelling

Protected By The Wolf Prince: A Red Riding Hood Retelling

Of Fate and Kings Series

Bound to the Dark Elf King

Claimed by the Dragon King

Taken by the Fae King

Stolen by the Wolf King

Captured by the Orc King

Of Gods and Fate (Greek God Romance Series)

Claimed By Hades

Bound to Ares

Orc Claimed Series

Claimed by the Orc

Of Dragons and Elves Series (Fantasy Romance)

The Elf Knight

Scarred Dragon Prince Series

<u>**Shadow Guard: Dragon Shifter Romance**</u>

To Love a Monster Book Series (Fantasy Romance)

<u>**Claimed by the Monster: A Monster Romance**</u>

V'loryn Holiday Series (A Marek and Elizabeth Holiday novella takes place prior to their bonding)

<u>**The Thing We Choose**</u>

V'loryn Fated Ones (Vampire Alien Romance)

<u>**Where the Light Begins (Vanek's Story)**</u>

Aerilon Fae Series (Fae Alien Romance)

<u>**Trace The Sky**</u> (Al'aneo's Story)

For information about upcoming releases Like me on

Facebook at <u>Jessica Grayson</u>

http://facebook.com/JessicaGraysonBooks.

OR

sign up for upcoming release alerts at my website:

Jessicagraysonauthor.com

Aria Winter

Thank you so much for reading this. I hope you enjoyed this story. If you enjoy my writing, I also write under the pen name *Jessica Grayson*.

For information about upcoming releases Like me on Facebook (<u>www.facebook.com/ariawinterauthor</u>) or sign up for upcoming release alerts at my website:

Want more Dragon Shifters? Check out my Beauty and the Beast Retelling below.

Once Upon A Fairy Tale Romance Series

Taken by the Dragon: A Beauty and the Beast Retelling

Captivated by the Fae: A Cinderella Retelling

Rescued By The Merman: A Little Mermaid Retelling

Bound to the Elf Prince: A Snow White Retelling

Elemental Dragon Warriors Series

Claimed by the Fire Dragon Prince

Stolen by the Wind Dragon Prince

Rescued by the Water Dragon Prince

Healed by the Earth Dragon Prince

Chosen By The Fire Dragon Guard

Saved By The Wind Dragon Guard

Treasured By The Water Dragon Guard

Taken By The Earth Dragon Guard

Cosmic Guardian Series

Charmed by the Fox's Heart

Seduced by the Peacock's Beauty

Protected by the Spider's Web

Ensnared by the Serpent's Gaze

Forged by the Dragon's Flame

Once Upon a Shifter Series

Ella and her Shifters

Snow White And Her Werewolves